"I'll Take Care Of You, Holly."

It was Connor's promise. If she carried his child he would ensure they both had the best of everything medicine and money had to offer.

"I can take care of myself." Holly lifted her chin in defiance at his words, yet her voice wavered. Her vulnerability cut Connor to the quick. What was he thinking? Had he been so addled by the intoxication of making love to her that he'd forgotten his position as her employer?

He dropped her hand as if her touch burned him.

"Holly, I—" He couldn't apologize for making love to her—especially when he wanted to do it again.

W9-AZJ-700

Dear Reader,

I've always considered myself extremely fortunate to have the unquestionable support and love of my family and have strived to re-create that sense of belonging with my own children. While growing up, I couldn't imagine how the holiday season must feel to those who have no one, especially those who don't even know where they come from.

From that flipside of my life Holly Christmas was born. Trying to imagine her unspeakable losses since babyhood, the steps to adulthood she could never share with family and her struggle to come to terms with who she is combined with her determination to discover her background reduced me to tears at times while writing this story, but I trust you'll find her path to happiness with Connor Knight as rewarding as she eventually does.

Of course, one passionate Knight brother is never enough, and I sincerely hope after reading Holly and Connor's story you'll look out for the next title in the NEW ZEALAND KNIGHTS series, *The CEO's Contract Bride* (on sale January 2007), where Connor's eldest and very sexy brother, Declan, meets his match.

With very best wishes,

Yvonne Lindsay

YVONNE LINDSAY

THE BOSS'S CHRISTMAS SEDUCTION

Silhouette® Desire

Published by Silhouette Books
America's Publisher of Contemporary Romance

If you purchased this book without a cover you should be aware
that this book is stolen property. It was reported as "unsold and
destroyed" to the publisher, and neither the author nor the
publisher has received any payment for this "stripped book."

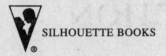

SILHOUETTE BOOKS

ISBN-13: 978-0-373-76758-8
ISBN-10:   0-373-76758-7

THE BOSS'S CHRISTMAS SEDUCTION

Copyright © 2006 by Yvonne Lindsay

All rights reserved. Except for use in any review, the reproduction
or utilization of this work in whole or in part in any form by any
electronic, mechanical or other means, now known or hereafter
invented, including xerography, photocopying and recording, or in
any information storage or retrieval system, is forbidden without
the written permission of the editorial office, Silhouette Books,
233 Broadway, New York, NY 10279 U.S.A.

All characters in this book have no existence outside the imagination of
the author and have no relation whatsoever to anyone bearing the same
name or names. They are not even distantly inspired by any individual
known or unknown to the author, and all incidents are pure invention.

This edition published by arrangement with Harlequin Books S.A.

® and TM are trademarks of Harlequin Books S.A., used under license.
Trademarks indicated with ® are registered in the United States Patent
and Trademark Office, the Canadian Trade Marks Office and in other
countries.

Visit Silhouette Books at www.eHarlequin.com

Printed in U.S.A.

YVONNE LINDSAY

New Zealand born, to Dutch immigrant parents, Yvonne Lindsay became an avid romance reader at the age of thirteen. Now, married to her "blind date" and with two surprisingly amenable teenagers, she remains a firm believer in the power of romance. Yvonne balances her days between a part-time legal management position and crafting the stories of her heart. In her spare time, when not writing, she can be found with her nose firmly in a book, reliving the power of love in all walks of life. She can be contacted via her Web site www.yvonnelindsay.com.

For Bron,
my mentor, my friend,

and

in memory of Delia Bridgens,
who introduced me to the joy of reading romance.

Thank you both for the impact you
have made on my life.

One

Bile rose in his throat. Hot, bitter, acrid bile.

Connor Knight dashed the investigator's report violently across the mahogany surface of his desk, scattering papers like giant confetti through the air where they hovered briefly, before floating to the thickly carpeted study floor.

Through the open French doors behind him he heard the drone of the launch's engines as it pulled away from his private jetty, taking the bearer of bad tidings back across the harbour to Auckland city.

The vile taste in Connor's mouth rivalled the malevolence of his ex-wife's actions. He swallowed against it, but the irrefutable proof of her betrayal could not be as easily diminished.

As if her insatiable partying and gambling hadn't been enough, now he knew that six months into their marriage she'd knowingly destroyed their baby—the child she knew he'd wanted—and had then been sterilised rather than ever bear another child again.

If not for a careless comment from one of her friends at a recent fund-raiser he'd have been none the wiser. Yet the throwaway remark had been all he needed to start the investigation and to confirm that she'd lied about the miscarriage.

A tearing pain clawed at his chest.

The proof of her treachery now lay scattered on his floor—information that had come at a hell of a price, but which was worth every last cent.

A copy of her admission to a private hospital four years ago, the bills from the anaesthetist, the surgeon, the hospital. The procedures. *Termination. Sterilisation.*

And through it all he'd been oblivious.

So now she wanted more money? He'd have paid it just to be rid of her—until he'd received today's information.

It had been bad enough to realise back then that she'd emasculated him with her deceit, her avaricious need to grasp at everything in her path during their brief union, but this? This went way further than that.

The grandfather clock chimed the hour. Nine o'clock. *Damn!* The meeting had made him later in to the office than he expected.

He punched the quick dial on the speakerphone on the desk, connecting immediately to his office in the city.

"Holly, I'm running late. Any messages or problems?"

"Nothing urgent, Mr. Knight, I've rescheduled your conference call to New York." His personal assistant's gentle, well-modulated voice washed over him like a calming wave of sanity in the madness of his morning. Thank goodness he could still rely on some people.

Connor slipped into his suit jacket, adjusted his tie and,

oblivious to the crunch of the report underfoot, stalked out the open French doors and towards the chopper waiting to take him from his island home and into Auckland's central business district.

If Holly Christmas received one more tartan-beribboned poinsettia she would scream.

So what if her birthday fell on Christmas Eve? She was used to that. After all, it *was* the same day every year. She blinked back the unbidden rush of tears that pricked her eyes, and gave herself a mental shake. Toughen up, she growled silently. Self-pity was so not her style. Survival—whatever it took—that was her key. Then why did she feel different this year? Empty. Alone.

At least her colleagues had remembered today was her birthday, and not just the last day of work before Knight Enterprises closed for the Christmas break. She straightened her shoulders, stiffened her spine and, with the plant clutched tightly to her aching chest, summoned a smile.

"The poinsettia is beautiful, thanks. I really appreciate it." The words sounded normal, thank goodness, coloured with just the right amount of enthusiasm.

"See you at the party tonight, Holly?" one of the girls asked.

"Oh, yes, I'll be there," she confirmed with a wry twist of her lips. Someone had to see to it that the annual bash ran smoothly, that the grossly inebriated were tactfully withdrawn from the proceedings and inserted into taxis and that spills and breakages were swiftly dealt with. For the third year in a row she was that someone.

She loved her job and she was darned good at it. No, she was better than good. She was the best. And that's why, after working her way through the secretarial pool here at Knight

Enterprises she'd risen to Executive PA to Connor Knight, head of the corporate law department.

A "ping" from the elevator bank down the hall heralded the tall, imposing figure striding along the carpet-lined corridor, and sent the small group of women scurrying back to their respective workstations. Holly turned and put the lush red-leafed poinsettia on the credenza behind her desk—next to the one from the finance department and the two that had come up from security and personnel. She caught her lower lip in between her teeth, tugging at its fullness. How on earth was she supposed to get them home on the bus?

"Good morning, Holly." His voice, as rich and dark as sinful chocolate, made the hairs on the back of her neck stand up. From the day she'd interviewed for her position as his personal assistant, her reaction to him had always been this painfully immediate, although she'd schooled herself to hide it well.

She'd given up asking herself why his presence made every nerve ending in her body stand on full alert, and learned instead to knuckle down and do her job, masking the flush of warmth that suffused her body. Some people didn't believe in love at first sight, but Holly knew from sudden and lasting experience that it happened.

She clenched her jaw slightly then slowly released it and the tension that bound her muscles, and turned to face him secure in the knowledge he'd never have an inkling as to the thoughts that raced through her mind or the sharpened awareness that brought her senses to screaming attention when he was around.

"Mr. Tanaka from the Tokyo office called about the negotiations. He sounded tense."

Connor didn't break his stride on his way through the open polished-rimu double doors that led to his corner office. "He must be. It's about five-thirty in the morning there. Get him on the line for me."

For the briefest moment Holly allowed herself the luxury of inhaling the lingering scent of his cologne—crisp, fresh and expensive yet with an underlying hint of something forbidden, especially to someone like her. With a mental shake she lifted the receiver of her phone, automatically punching in the numbers that would connect his private line to Japan. She waited until he picked up, then she stood to unlatch the hooks that held the doors open to his interior office. Absorbed in the conversation, his Japanese flawless, he didn't so much as acknowledge her.

Holly indulged in a tiny sigh. Well, love at first sight on her part or not, Connor Knight was oblivious. Newly divorced from his socialite wife when Holly had started working for him, he'd looked right through her, and every other woman who'd crossed his path since, as if she didn't exist. She was a highly dependable machine to him, period.

Confident the call with Mr. Tanaka would tie him up for some time, she made one last check through the details for the staff and children's Christmas parties. This year she'd excelled herself. The cafeteria, transformed into a fairy grotto, looked stunning, and at six-thirty Connor would be playing Santa Claus.

A wry smile played around Holly's lips as she eyed the glaring red Santa suit that hung on the antique brass hat stand in the corner. Mr. Knight, Sr. had insisted Connor play Santa this year, claiming his arthritic knee made it difficult for him to attend to the task, and saying how important it was someone from the family took on the role. Oh, Connor had argued against it, but once his father made up his mind there was no denying it—especially not from his youngest son.

It was probably the only time she'd witnessed her boss at a total disadvantage.

"Hell." A deep voice from behind made her spin around in her chair. "He doesn't really expect me to wear that, does he?"

"I think you'll make a wonderful Santa, Mr. Knight."

The disgust on his face was self-evident. He thrust a dicta-tape at her together with a clutch of papers. "Transcribe this for me straight away. Oh, and before you do, check the boardroom is free and tell the team we need to meet in half an hour."

"Trouble?" Holly enquired, mentally shifting his appointments to free him up for the rest of the morning. It had to be serious if the whole legal team was being called in.

"Nothing we can't handle. Timing's a bit of a blow, though." He cast a baleful glance at the Santa suit, draped limply on the hanger. "I don't suppose…"

"He's not going to let you get out of it." She shook her head sympathetically.

"No, he won't." Connor huffed out a breath and pushed a hand through his immaculately cut and styled hair, sending several strands into unaccustomed disarray.

Holly stifled another smile. This whole Santa thing had sent the cool, calm and sophisticated Connor Knight for a loop, and this from a man she'd seen face down battalions of international lawyers over land and property deals.

She'd never have dreamed that the prospect of a steady procession of children queuing to take their turn seated on his knee would elicit such a nervous response. Still, who was she to ponder? Children made her nervous, too, and, unlike so many of her peers, Holly had put her biological clock firmly on hold. At twenty-six the rest of her life stretched long and lonely ahead of her. There'd be no kids in her future, at least not until she had some answers about her past.

She hated this time of year. All the fun and gaiety of the

festivities served to remind her of everything she didn't have—had never had. Knowing she'd ensured everyone else's fun tonight would have to be sufficient to buoy her through the harrowing, bleak emptiness of the holiday break until she could bury herself back in work.

Holly sighed again, and bent to the task at hand. Regretting her decision was not a possibility. Maybe she'd grow old in this chair, or one just like it in another office in another city, but she'd be the best executive PA on the planet. That would have to be enough.

Shrieks of laughter echoed around the room as the clown she'd hired made a fool of himself yet again. Holly took a quick look at her watch. Five minutes until Santa time. He should be here by now. Maybe he was having trouble with the suit.

She turned to her assistant, Janet, a quiet young woman not long out of business college but already showing every sign of making a great PA herself in time.

"If I'm not back in five minutes with Mr. Knight, give the clown the nod to carry on a little longer, will you?"

"Is there anything else I can do to help?"

"No, I'm sure we'll be fine. Santa probably got a phone call."

In the elevator Holly mentally ticked off the order of the evening, everything *had* to run like clockwork. Irritation drummed at the back of her mind. As much as she sympathised with Connor's reluctance to play Santa tonight, he had an obligation to the kids. An obligation he had no business putting off. If he'd bailed on those excited children downstairs she'd be giving him a piece of her mind, boss or not.

She covered the distance from the elevator bank to his corner office in record time and knocked sharply before pushing through the doors. The head of anger she'd built up propelled her into his office with a flurry. But her words stalled in her throat, and she halted midstride.

Connor Knight stood, half-dressed, in the middle of his office. The garish red trousers of his suit hung loosely on his hips, threatening to drop lower if he so much as moved a muscle.

Holly dragged her eyes upwards, her throat as dry as the Sahara, and a deep-seated throb pulsed through her body. Lord have mercy, she thought as her gaze swept across the disturbingly bare tanned expanse of his chest, to the powerful width of his shoulders above it and to the strong column of his neck. It was amazing what Armani could hide, she thought as she forced herself to look him in the eye, hoping the surge of energy that rocketed with heated awareness through her wasn't apparent on her face. If her internal temperature was anything to go by, she should be glowing like a beacon.

She took a steadying breath. What was she here for again? Oh, yes, that's right. Santa.

"Five minutes, Mr. Knight."

"Yeah, I know. Damn suit's too big. Help me stuff some cushions in here. I'm sure the kids of today still expect a bit of meat on their Santas."

"I imagine so," she agreed, and swept up an armful of cushions from the sofa in his office. "Will these do?" she asked.

"As good as anything. Here," Connor slid his hands behind the band of the trousers and held them away from his waist. "You stuff, I'll hold."

He had to be joking. Holly hesitated and swallowed against the constriction in her throat.

"What are you waiting for?" He shot her a glance, a tiny frown pulling his dark brows together briefly, his impatience clear.

Of course he had no idea of his effect on her. To him she wasn't a woman with needs and desires. She was just his PA.

Besides, as his PA, why wouldn't she be called upon to stuff cushions in her boss's trousers?

"I suppose this is what you meant in my job description, when you said 'and other duties as required from time to time.'" Keep it light she told herself. Just keep it light.

Surprise skated over his features at her words. Holly inwardly groaned. Why on earth had she said that?

His eyes suddenly crinkled at the edges and he laughed—a rusty sound, as if he didn't do it often enough. "Yeah, something like that. Although, I don't think HR had this scenario in mind."

Holly returned a nervous smile and forced herself forward. Warmth radiated from his bare torso, or was that just the flush of heat in her cheeks? She fought to quell the tremor that threatened to vibrate through her and, with a stern silent warning to herself not to look down, she carefully eased the first cushion between his ridged abdomen and the red satin.

"It's okay, Holly. I won't bite."

Oh, great. Now he was laughing at her. Fine, she'd show him she wasn't scared. She shoved in the next cushion with more haste than finesse, her fingers accidentally grazing against the fine row of dark hair that feathered from his belly button and down. She heard the hitch in his breathing as she touched him and snatched her hand back as goose bumps rose on his skin.

"That should do the trick." Darn, was that a quaver in her voice? Worse, had he heard it?

"I need more."

More? Her hand still burned from its fleeting touch against his skin—the texture of the hair beneath his belly button a tactile impression against her fingers—she needed more, too, although she knew with painful honesty they weren't thinking about the same thing.

With her lower lip caught between her teeth, Holly edged

another cushion into the waistband. The urge to let her fingers linger against the heated surface of his belly tempted her like a candy shop window did a sugar addict. Determined not to give in to her baser instincts she gave the padded mass a gentle, dehumanising pat. "There, that's it."

She reached for the red jacket, yanked it off its hanger and held it out for him. She allowed herself the brief luxury of letting her gaze stroke across his back and shoulders, mesmerised by the play of his muscles as he shrugged into the garment and cinched the broad, black belt around his now-expanded waistline.

He grabbed the hat and beard from his desk and hastily arranged them before turning to face Holly again.

"So, how do I look?"

Her breath caught. How did he look? She blinked, searching for the words to describe him. He certainly wasn't like the Santas that had filled her with terror as a child, and caused her to drag free of her caregiver's hand to tearfully hasten as far away as she could get.

Despite the padding at his waist and the ridiculously fluffy beard that obscured the strong lines of his jaw, she couldn't erase the half-naked picture of him that burned on her retinas. She barely trusted herself to speak.

"You've forgotten the eyebrows," she eventually managed. Well done, she congratulated herself, that almost sounded like her usual cool, composed self.

"I don't have to wear those white caterpillars, do I?"

"Of course you do, you wouldn't be Santa without them."

Holly clenched and unclenched her fingers in a vain attempt to stem the trembling that threatened to give away her nerves before she peeled the stick-on brows from the backing paper. She leaned nearer and reached up to smooth them above his eyes, trying desperately not to let her fingers linger on his face. He bent his head slightly to assist, and suddenly his lips were level with hers—the warmth of his breath caressing her cheek.

So close, yet so far. All she had to do was step in, just one tiny step, and press her lips against his. To give life to the dreams that invaded her sleep and caused her to wake, tangled in her sheets, filled with a want she could never assuage.

Hastily she quelled her rampant thoughts and concentrated on applying the strips of white fluff. She'd be on the fast track to unemployment if she gave in to her desires, and no way could she afford that. Not with Andrea's medical fees to consider. The reminder was as chilling as an Antarctic winter.

Finally, the job done, she stepped away to safety—to where she couldn't give in to impulse. "You look great," she said softly.

"Well then, that's all that matters. Let's go."

They travelled in silence to the eighth-floor cafeteria where Holly put a steadying hand on his red sleeve. She tried to ignore the waves of heat that emanated through the fabric to her fingers.

"Wait here," she ordered, although her voice came out like a strangled croak and earned her a strange look from the dark eyes that burned under bushy white brows. "I need to let your warm-up act announce you first."

Was it her imagination or had he suddenly become paler? Surely he wasn't scared? Not Connor Knight. Under the fluffy beard, she discerned small lines of tension bracketing his lips, and the urge to comfort him stilled her in her tracks.

"You'll be fine," she murmured softly, as reassuringly as she could. "The kids will love you."

"You're staying, aren't you?"

His question caught her by surprise. She hadn't planned on

sticking around for this part of the proceedings. Seeing a line of children waiting to sit with Santa still had the power to fill her with dread.

"No, I have some other things to attend to. I'll be back just before the party finishes."

"Stay."

Holly looked away. He had no idea. But then, of course, why should he? Everyone loved Christmas. Everyone but the little girl who'd grown up saddled with a surname chosen by Social Services that linked her irrevocably to the most traumatic experience of her life. It was one of the reasons she never disclosed her background or years in foster care. No one wanted to admit they'd been abandoned. As far as Holly was concerned, her life had begun the day she'd turned eighteen and been released from the state's control.

"Holly?"

Her teeth were clenched so hard she was amazed they didn't shatter in her jaw, and her throat ached with years of suppressed tension. She couldn't explain, not even to him. Some things you kept buried. She gave him a tight nod. "Let's get it over with."

The children didn't give him the slightest opportunity to be nervous. Their vigorous excitement and squeals of pleasure energised the room to such an extent Holly felt as though her nerves would shred into ribbons and scatter all around her. Why on earth had she agreed to stay? It was madness.

Seated on his special throne, Connor lifted a little girl with a gleaming cap of dark hair onto his lap. The child, no more than three or four, scanned the room, her bottom lip starting to tremble.

Despite the constant temperature of air conditioning, tiny beads of perspiration prickled along Holly's spine. A wave of dizziness made her press her body against the hard wall behind her—trying to connect with something solid, something real. Anything other than the dread that built within her and threatened to swamp her mind. She dragged a deep breath into deflated lungs, struggling to push the fear back down—down to where she could control it—but it was too late.

An image flashed, sharp and clear in her mind, and in a heartbeat she was lost. She was that little girl. Sitting on Santa's knee, her eyes nervously—futilely—raking the crowd of shoppers for her mother. Nervousness becoming fear. Fear becoming absolute terror when she couldn't find her mother's face anywhere in the swirling mass.

The authorities had been summoned as soon as someone could make any sense out of her hysterical sobbing. But not quickly enough to find her mother in the crowd of stunned onlookers. Even now the overwhelming sense of desertion and loss left Holly shocked and vulnerable.

Resentment lanced through her, swift and searing, before she determinedly crushed it. She'd given up trying to work out what kind of mother walked away from her child the night before Christmas—abandoning a three-year-old to strangers and an uncertain future.

She forced herself to find an anchor, something she could focus on and that would help her bring her rapid breathing back under control and calm the tremors that shook her frame. That anchor was Connor Knight as, with infinite patience, he pointed out the little girl's parents in the crowd and cajoled a smile from her worried wee face.

Holly uncurled her fisted hands, feeling the sharp sting of sensation as blood eked its way back to her fingertips. Across the room the little girl was smiling and waving to her mother. And Connor, instead of paying attention to the child on his lap, was staring straight back at her. She watched as his lips, outlined by the absurdly fluffy beard, framed the words, "Are you all right?" Had he noticed her panic? She gave a weak smile and lifted her chin with a small nod. He held her gaze a moment longer, then turned his attention back to the child in his care and handed her a cheerfully wrapped gift.

This was how it was meant to be for kids. Each one with their own special gift and a chance to impart their deepest desires for Christmas morning to Santa, and the steady assurance of a loving parent waiting in the wings. Hadn't she wished that for herself so many times?

When the last parcel was distributed, it was time to call the children's party to an end. Santa had other obligations, and Holly's half-hour window between the children's party and the staff party was closing.

With a small announcement she brought the celebrations to a close and judging by the overwhelming round of applause, from both parents and children, Connor was a hit. As everyone filtered out, Holly finally allowed herself to relax, the knot of tension that kept her operating at maximum performance efficiency all day, all year for that matter, slowly untangling. Only one more party to get through, then it was all over for another year, she consoled herself.

"What was that all about?" Connor Knight's voice slid through her like a hot knife through butter.

She drew in a long breath before answering. "I think it went well, don't you? The children certainly loved you."

"You looked like you'd seen a ghost."

Holly sighed. Evasion wouldn't work. Tenacity was one of the many talents that had driven him to being one of the most-respected men in his field—worldwide. He wouldn't give up until completely satisfied with her answer.

"Just catching my breath. That's all. It's taken a bit of work, getting this all organised." She tried to assure him, and for a moment thought she'd succeeded.

A tiny flash lit the onyx depths of his eyes and grew into the hot glow of challenge. "Looked like more than that to me. I thought you were going to keel over."

"Oh, good heavens, no." Holly forced a smile on her face.

"Are you okay now?" he persisted.

"I'm fine. Just fine."

"You've been pushing yourself too hard. Janet will take over for this evening."

"No, I'm okay. Truly."

Connor gave her a hard look. "We'll see about that. Come on, we'd better get ready for the next onslaught."

"You go on ahead. I'll meet you back down here."

She watched as he left. What had made him notice her during that dreadful moment of weakness? Had anyone else seen it? She should never have agreed to stay on. Never.

Holly quickly glanced around. The cleaning staff were busy completing the transformation of the children's party to a more sophisticated reenactment of a Christmas fantasy. It had been a brainwave to carry through the same delightful childlike theme to the staff party, and such a simple solution, given the time constraints. She wasn't needed here any longer.

Back upstairs in her office, Holly opened the coat cupboard and lifted a long dry cleaner's carrier from the rail. It was a simple matter to slip into the ladies' room to change and touch up her makeup. She took a brief minute to loosen her hair, combing through its thick dark length so hard her scalp tingled. She studied her reflection a moment. How long had it been since she'd let her hair down, literally or figuratively?

Too long. But time was not a commodity she could afford to waste. Not when so much depended on her.

She twisted her hair back up again, softening the tight twist that she usually wore by securing the silky black length in a fuller, softer knot at the nape of her neck. Finally satisfied when not a hair dared stray out of place she slicked on a ruby-coloured lipstick. The sales assistant had been right, Holly acceded with a small grimace, the rich colour did bring life to her faintly olive-tinted skin. She preferred softer, more understated colours that wouldn't draw attention to the fullness of her lips, yet knew that she needed something striking for this evening. Besides, she'd reminded herself, today was her birthday. A girl had a right to look good.

A swift glance at her watch reminded her she had little time left. Holly slipped out of her sombre businesslike suit and carefully unzipped the carrier to remove the ankle-length crimson sheath cocooned within.

The high, straight, boat neckline of the sleeveless gown belied the deep vee cut away at its back. Holly unhooked her bra and stuffed it in the bottom of the carrier bag before stepping into the gown and shimmying the silky lined fabric up over her body. Surveying her reflection in the mirror, she wondered if she hadn't gone too far this year; normally she hired a black dress, but there was something about this gown that had beckoned to her like a promise of hidden treasure. She'd hesitated at the cost, mindful of her financial commitments, but it wasn't as if she'd be deluged with gifts from family or a lover. She had neither.

So for once she'd splurged. This was her gift to herself, and she would bask in the pleasure of wearing the gown all evening.

The minute Holly stepped from the ladies' room she heard a raised female voice through the open door to Connor's office.

She would have recognised his ex-wife's shrill tone anywhere. Before the divorce the secretarial pool had been at her beck and call to assist with her charity work—Carla Knight was nothing if not demanding. The girls would draw straws before anyone would set foot on this floor to take her instructions. Holly sent a silent wish skywards that whatever the situation was, and it sounded intense, it would be resolved quickly.

As silently as she could, she stowed her things back in her cupboard and turned to leave when suddenly Connor's voice vibrated through the air, disgust lacing his words with a sharpness Holly had rarely heard from him.

"You don't deny it then?"

"How dare you have me investigated? Those records were private!"

"Everything has its price, Carla. Unfortunately I never realised yours until it was too late. You can tell your fancy overpriced divorce lawyer you won't be getting another cent beyond the settlement you've already received. Ever. Now, get out of my sight."

"Gladly!"

It was too late to retreat now. Holly straightened her shoulders. There was nothing else for it but to meet the former Mrs. Knight face on.

"Slumming it with the staff tonight, Connor?" Carla spat, vitriol poisoning her exquisite features as she pushed her petite frame past Holly. She slanted a spiteful glare at Holly. "I might have known you'd be hovering around. But of course, I forgot, you don't have anyone to go home to, do you?"

Speechless, Holly stood back and let the other woman through, leaving behind her a cloud of expensive French fragrance and the air crackling with ill humour.

"I'm sorry you had to bear the brunt of that, Holly."

She drew in a calming breath and turned to face him. Connor stood at the door to his office, the usual resonance in his voice flat, his eyes glittering and fired with anger.

"It's all right, sir." She reached across her desk and extracted her evening bag from the top drawer, determined not to acknowledge the barb Carla had flung. She refused to submit to the other woman's cruel taunt; she'd grown up with worse. While such sneers had the power to inflict pain, Holly had learned the hard way to never let it show. She straightened from her desk. "Are you ready to go back downstairs?"

He let out a breath, slowly and carefully, as if he'd been holding on to his control by a thread.

"Yeah. I'm ready." He took a step towards her and let out a low whistle. "And so, it appears, are you." A feral flash of hunger blazed and died in his eyes so quickly Holly wondered if she'd identified it correctly. "Holly, you look…amazing."

She forced herself to remember to breathe as he raked her body with his eyes. It was one thing being the target of a few harshly spoken words, but quite another to be the target of a gaze that stroked her body like a silk scarf over bare skin. It was as if he saw her through new eyes. She instantly pushed the idea away for the foolishness it was.

"Thank you, sir. You look pretty amazing yourself." Formal dress should make a man look more distant, she decided distractedly, not make him look so wickedly sensual. With his dark hair and eyes, and dressed in a tailored black suit with a crisp white shirt and black bow tie at his tanned throat, Connor Knight looked like he'd stepped out of a dream fantasy. *Her* dream fantasy. The one where they stood at an altar and he promised to love and cherish her, forever. *Enough!* Holly snapped her thoughts back into the present. To reality.

She turned her back on him and began to walk towards the

door before she did or said anything foolish. Her emotions had already taken a battering tonight, and the way he looked, not to mention the way he looked at her, scrambled her senses so badly she could barely think let alone walk straight.

"Hold on a minute, Holly." His voice came from close behind. "Shall we?" He offered his arm and, with only a tiny hesitation, she threaded her hand through the crook of his elbow and laid her fingers on his sleeve. He was a solid wall of strength next to her, his hip brushing against hers with each step as he matched his pace to hers. Holly's nerves wound tighter and tighter, like a spring about to snap.

In the elevator she found respite by removing her hand from his arm and stepping slightly away to press the button to take them back downstairs. She let her hand drop back down to her side, where it rested momentarily before Connor's strong fingers grasped hers and replaced them on his sleeve.

"Mr Knight?" Her voice caught on a tiny gasp.

His eyes burned with an emotion she couldn't quite tag. One corner of his mouth tilted, almost as if he mocked himself. "Humour me, Holly. Maybe I need a beautiful woman on my arm tonight."

Two

Lost for words, Holly tried to school her features into their usual calm. Yet when her eyes met his, she couldn't hold his gaze, and they flicked nervously instead to her fingers lying, starkly docile, against the black cloth of his tuxedo. He needed her? That was an entirely new and unexpected development. One she wasn't sure how to handle.

Beneath her hand she sensed the play of muscles in his forearm. Suppressed tension shimmered off him in waves. Okay, so he was stinging after his meeting with Carla, and maybe he was using her for whatever reason tonight—she could accept that—but try as she might, it was difficult to subdue the answering call of her body to the leashed power of his. Heat flickered deep inside her, tiny flames taking hold and sending burning liquid through her veins.

Need? She knew all about need.

As short as the elevator ride was, to Holly it felt like

forever. If they didn't make the distance soon she was certain she'd melt, lose her inhibitions and press herself against his tensely held form.

The cooling air of the cafeteria was a breath of sanity as the doors opened. Staff and their partners had already begun to arrive and were drifting around the room in a hum of conversation.

Connor wondered how long it would be before he could shuck his duties and slink back to his flat. A couple of hours, tops. Holly needed to take it easy, too. She'd scared him tonight when he'd looked across the room and seen her face, as stark and white as the wall behind her, during the children's party. Despite her denial, it was obvious something was wrong.

It didn't stop you using her to make yourself feel better, a cynical voice from inside remarked with scathing honesty. The admission brought him down a notch. No, he hadn't hesitated. Holly was the antithesis of the vicious blazing fury of Carla's indignation—the constant epitome of calm in his storm. An influence, he freely admitted, he'd always taken for granted.

Until he'd seen her tonight, and been hurriedly and disturbingly reminded she was most definitely a woman. A sensuously beautiful woman.

He looked at the slender bow of her neck as she fussed with something in her evening bag and wondered how her skin would feel, would taste. Connor clamped a lid on the thought before it had time to flourish and grow into something more than a tingle of awareness. She was his PA. And she'd be horrified if she knew the rampant slant of his thoughts. No doubt she'd be a darn sight paler than she'd been earlier tonight.

There was a flush on her cheeks now, he noted with some relief, and her eyes, as they darted about the room checking everything, had a sparkle in their blue depths that had been missing before. He was glad he'd made the decision earlier to put Janet in charge of tonight. Holly deserved the break, and her assistant had been thrilled at the chance to show off her training. It was a win-win all round, and it would keep Holly at his side—all night.

Connor bent his head close to her ear. "Relax, Holly, you're officially off duty as of now." Her faint scent teased his nostrils with its hint of warm summer nights and fresh linen, and enticed him to linger before his own hands-off rule, lit in neon signs across the back of his eyes.

"But someone has to oversee—"

"I've instructed Janet to take over for you tonight, she'll manage fine. You've organised the party to within a nanosecond of perfection, anyway. Let her take care of whatever crops up."

"Really, I must—"

"Relax," he urged her quietly.

With his dark head still bent to hers so intimately, he realised they were getting speculative glances from a few of the staff around the room. The office buzz needed little to fuel it, although most wouldn't dare get caught out in gossip about one of the Knights. He needed to get things back on an even footing, although for some indeterminate reason he didn't want to.

"You must let me do my job," she protested again, taking a tiny step away.

Connor fought back a frustrated retort. He elegantly snagged two glasses of champagne from a passing waiter and pressed one into her fingers. "Your job is done, Holly. Here, celebrate. Another brilliant year, thank you." He clinked his glass gently against hers in his own personal toast.

"You know I don't drink at company functions."

"Quit arguing and lighten up, hmm?" He scanned the room. "Try to look as though you're having fun. I insist." He lowered his voice and gave her a mock-stern glower. For a moment he thought she'd taken him seriously, until a welcome spark of rebellion flared in her eyes, darkening and deepening their intense blue.

Had he ever noticed the colour of her eyes before tonight? He must have, surely. The negative response, as he dredged his memory, reminded him of his position, and hers. Of course he hadn't paid attention to her features. Then why, he wondered, did he want more detail tonight?

A perverse, devilish urge made him shift closer to her as the revellers swirled about them, and he placed his free hand against her exposed lower back. Under his fingers her spine straightened, ramrod stiff, as he stroked lightly across skin that felt astonishingly heated. The contrast between his cool fingers and her intense warmth reminded him yet again of their differences, their positions, urging him to desist while sensation burned an enticing brand across his fingertips. He sensed, rather than heard, Holly's breath catch in her throat. This was getting out of control. *He* was getting out of control, and way overstepping the mark.

Reluctantly he withdrew his hand. Just in time it seemed, as Janet came over, gushing with pride. "You don't need to worry, Holly, I have it all under control. I think Mr. Knight's idea to let you enjoy yourself tonight was great, don't you? For once you can be one of the guests and really have a good time."

Holly's lips peeled back from her teeth in what approximated a smile but inside she was on the verge of shattering.

"Thank you, Janet. I…I appreciate you stepping into the breach like that. But don't hesitate to—"

"You're doing a marvellous job, Janet. Thank you." Connor's fingers stroked another delicious line across the small of her back, sending a cascade of goose bumps rippling beneath the seam of her gown and shocking the words she was about to utter into silence.

She couldn't stand it anymore. She stepped forward and turned so he could no longer reach her bare skin. 'Mr. Knight—"

"Connor. And let it go for one night, okay. Orders from the boss." He stared down the final protest that hovered on her lips, a taunting slant to his smile. "Speaking of the boss, let's work our way over and see mine." He nodded to where his father, Tony Knight, the founder and president of Knight Enterprises stood, like the patriarch he was, his erect posture exuding strength and pride as he gazed about the room.

The steady gentle pressure of Connor's hand returned against the base of her spine, a pressure that sent wild spirals of warmth unfurling through her body. She barely acknowledged the greetings and festive wishes from the staff as they cut a swathe through the crowd, the minglers parting like the Red Sea as they moved across the room.

As they neared the gathering of senior executives, she struggled to regain her composure, to ignore the imprint of Connor's proprietary hand against the small of her back and to settle the butterflies that fluttered every time she had to deal with the senior Mr. Knight. She worked with men of his position and power on a regular basis, but there was something about Antony Knight that commanded respect. A respect that, for Holly, bordered on something closer to awe. She certainly didn't want to dissolve like an idiot at his feet because his youngest son was sending her senses into meltdown.

A first generation Kiwi, born to Italian immigrant parents who'd anglicised their name to better fit into their adopted country, Tony Knight had built Knight Enterprises from the ground up. Holly had no doubt he could still swing a hammer with the best of them, but that wasn't what made her admire him the most.

No, she acknowledged as she fought to bank the fire burning in her veins, it was his unstinting devotion to his family. His abiding love for his long-dead wife. He'd raised three sons while building an empire, and yet, even though she had no doubt that the past had been rocky, he'd maintained that solid thread of familial connection between them. Despite his setbacks he hadn't given them up to strangers to raise, like her mother had when she'd discarded Holly, as if she'd been unwanted baggage.

Holly would give just about anything to be a part of a background like that. A background she could call her own. The sobering thought did its work with chilling accuracy and she stepped clear of Connor's reach to greet his father.

Her face ached with the effort of keeping a smile pasted on.

Connor had stayed close to her all evening, shepherding her as she mingled and chatted sociably with their colleagues, ensuring she constantly had a glass of champagne in her fingers and that she stayed well clear of administrative responsibilities for the evening. For once she knew what it felt like to be the one being looked after—the sensation was totally foreign to her and strangely unsettling at the same time.

She lifted her drink to her lips and took a tiny sip of the wine. Darn, warm again. She'd barely drunk a full glass all evening. Mind you, that was probably a good thing. Her stomach had been so knotted with tension she hadn't eaten, either. While the food on the buffet and circulating on trays looked wonderful, and as usual she'd ensured there was plenty of it, she simply couldn't bring herself to take a bite.

She flicked a glance to the wall clock by the door, and her shoulders sagged gently in relief. Things would draw to a close soon. Mr. Knight, Sr. would make his usual end-of-year speech, thanking the skeleton crew who would keep the business ticking over in its usual efficient fashion during the three weeks while most staff took their holiday break, and wishing everyone a happy Christmas.

Happy Christmas indeed, for those who had family and friends to share it with. Holly felt a tiny frown pull at her forehead, and the beginnings of a headache prodded behind her eyes.

Would Andrea even be aware it was Christmas Day tomorrow? The staff at the nursing home had recommended that Holly not come in, and that her foster sister wouldn't worry if for once she spent a holiday with her other friends. Except Holly had no one else she wanted to spend the day with. Andrea was all she had—her one positive link to her past.

Maybe she'd call into the home, anyway, and take Andrea the filmy new nightgown she'd bought her—a soft mossy green, to match her eyes.

"Hey, smile. It's Christmas, remember? No need to look so sad." Connor's warm breath caressed the side of her neck, his voice lowered to a sensuous hum that stroked along her nerve endings like fingertips over plush velvet. A rush of awareness prickled all the way up into her scalp.

"Was I?" She turned to face him. "I'm okay."

"Are you sure?"

"Of course," she responded in her usual brisk tone.

"Good to see you're feeling better." Connor grinned back at her. "You've got your 'office voice' back again. Come on, let your hair down. Enjoy yourself."

"I am." Oh, Lord, she sounded so darn prim and defensive.

To offset the prudishly proper tone of her voice she lifted her wine again to take another sip, but was halted when a warm hand grasped her wrist. A shock of electricity raced up to her hand, causing a wild tremble as Connor took the glass from her suddenly nerveless fingers.

"Here, I'll get you another. That one must be warm by now. You *are* supposed to drink it, you know."

She shook her head slightly, but he ignored her and signalled to a passing waiter for a fresh glass. She grasped the slender stem, sloshing a bit of the wine over the edge.

"Are you sure you're all right, Holly?" Connor stepped closer, his arm slipping supportively behind her back. "You still look a bit shaky, there."

"I'm fine. Just a little tired, that's all. If you don't mind, perhaps I could slip away early."

"Great idea." Connor scanned the room. "I think we've done our dash tonight. Let's go."

Together?

"No, truly," she protested, "you stay. I'm sure your father—"

"Will excuse me this time. He owes me for that Santa episode. He knows how I feel about kids." Even though he was smiling, there was a hard glitter in his eyes. The urbane mask he'd worn all evening slipped, and bleakness hardened his face to marble.

"You don't like children?" Holly couldn't keep the surprise from her voice. He'd been so natural with the little ones, so patient.

"On the contrary." His voice was clipped. "He knows exactly how much children mean to me. Let's make our good-byes." He slipped her hand in the crook of his arm, and they moved to where his father was holding court with a bunch of his cronies. She felt every eye in the room surreptitiously staring at them as they cut through the crowd.

What on earth was he talking about? If he liked children, why the big deal about being Santa? Unless, a thought occurred to her with sharpening clarity, it had served as a painful reminder of what he didn't have. That might explain his reluctance earlier tonight, not to mention his irritation with his dad.

Another gulf of difference between them. He wanted kids; she didn't. So don't go getting any ideas about his behaviour tonight, she warned herself firmly.

"I see the two of you are off, then." Tony Knight sent a sharp look at Connor, which Holly read quite clearly as admonishment. She watched the silent interplay between father and son, neither backing down, yet an undercurrent so strong flowing between them no one would dare get caught in their crossfire. Holly knew Tony Knight frowned on relationships between staff, and for the life of her she couldn't understand why Connor was giving his father the impression they were leaving together.

"Yes, Papa. *We* are."

Connor's subtle emphasis on the word *we* made the older man's lips thin somewhat in response, and his eyes flicked assessingly between her and his youngest son. A frisson of disquiet trickled down Holly's spine. He thought they were a couple? She had to dissuade him from that idea straight away.

Before she could interject, he bent down and bussed Holly's cheeks in his extravagant Italian fashion. Her shock at his action burst through her cool reserve, painting a warm stain of colour on her face. For all that his family had done their best to adopt the "Kiwi way", he was, and would always remain, Italian to the soles of his handmade shoes.

"You did a marvellous job again tonight, Holly." He smiled,

although it didn't quite reach his eyes. They remained sharply tuned to her face—watching as intently as a hawk, and making her feel about as vulnerable as a field mouse exposed on an overgrazed paddock.

"It's my pleasure, sir," she eventually managed, her own smile frozen on her face.

He gave a sharp nod in acknowledgement, then fired his gaze back at Connor. "I'll still be seeing you tomorrow morning, then? Remember my cousin Isabella and her daughter will also be attending."

"Of course." She felt Connor's arm tighten beneath the fine cloth of his suit as if he was holding himself in check.

"Good." His father turned slightly, dismissing them both.

"I thought I'd invite Holly to join us. You don't mind, do you?" Connor's challenge hung in the air, and he faced down the shocked expression on his father's face. He turned to Holly. "You don't have any plans for the morning do you?"

"But I—" she began to protest.

"I'm sure Holly—" Tony Knight spoke simultaneously.

Connor raised an eyebrow at Holly. "Well?"

"I can't intrude."

"So you have no plans, then, for tomorrow?"

"No." Her response was barely a breath on the air. She hated having to admit it. Hated it, and the unwanted sympathy it always engendered, with a vengeance.

"Fine. We'll be there at ten-thirty, Papa."

Holly felt as though she'd been hijacked. At what point had Connor decided to use her in some game he was playing against his father? And why? The older man's eyes were spitting chips of ice although he reined in his anger well. If she hadn't already been so finely attuned to the atmosphere between the two men, she might not even have noticed.

"Don't be late." Tony Knight bit off the command, acceding he'd been outmanoeuvred.

"We won't be."

Before she could further analyse their veiled animosity, Connor was guiding her towards the door.

In the elevator Connor released a deep sigh and leaned back against the wall, closing his eyes briefly. He was sick of playing his father's games. Tony Knight had tried to control each of his three boys at some time or another. Connor had always counted his blessings that he'd been last in the queue. But tonight, especially tonight, he'd resolved not to play his father's game any longer. There was no way he'd be put on parade for yet another matchmaking attempt with yet another distant cousin. The pressure his old man had been exerting, initially subtle and then later not so, for Connor to get over Carla and find a new woman to make a home—a family—with, had been the last straw. Especially today.

He shouldn't have used Holly like that, though. It was shameful. He'd seen the questions flinging around in his father's mind as if they were graffiti, starkly spray painted on the boardroom wall. What was he, Connor, thinking? Christmas had always traditionally been for family. Only family. The last woman he'd brought had been Carla, as his wife. He knew he'd be in for a grilling tomorrow. What the hell? It'd be worth it. Maybe he'd even get around to telling his father about the grandchild he'd never get to know or love.

He glanced at Holly. The slender line of her throat arched slightly as she held her head tilted, staring at the numbers as they lit consecutively on the overhead console. A man could dream about making love to a neck like that. Feathering gentle kisses along the pale-blue pulse that beat beneath her ear.

Stroking his tongue down the feminine cord of her neck, lower and lower until he bit softly at the curve of her shoulder.

Heat flooded his groin, driving his body to full, pulsing life. What the hell was he thinking? Holly wasn't some potential conquest to reignite the flame of hunger his wife had annihilated with her deceptions. Yet, for some reason he couldn't tear his eyes from her throat, and his mouth dried as he imagined living out the fantasy of the image playing in his mind.

At their floor, the doors slid smoothly open and she stepped out ahead of him, affording him a delectable view of her smooth straight back. Her skin glowed with a hint of colour that made him wonder if she'd be that colour all over.

A jolt of need struck him, deep and hard. Suddenly, Lord help him, it was crucial to find out.

Three

"It always feels weird being here when everyone's gone home." Holly retrieved her suit carrier and handbag from the cupboard in her office.

"Yeah," Connor agreed from where he leaned against the wall, his hands thrust into his trouser pockets.

Holly turned, startled by the odd note to his voice. He watched her, his dark black-brown eyes unblinking. The burning heat in them made her stomach lurch with a nervous flip-flop.

She needed to get this business about Christmas Day sorted now. "About tomorrow—"

"I'll pick you up in the morning. I'll need your address."

He pushed off the wall and came to stand closer. The fresh citrus scent of his cologne together with the underlying spice of pure male filled her nostrils. They flared involuntarily, as if trying to inhale his scent deeper. Instantaneously she shut down the urge to breathe in deep, switching instead to short, shallow intakes through her mouth. It was one thing to believe yourself in love with your boss but quite another to believe he was interested in return. Somehow he must have unconsciously picked up the message that she was attracted to him, more than attracted if her wildly chaotic hormones were anything to go by. He was strong, he was male, no doubt he was reacting instinctively to whatever signals she'd been sending. The signals had to stop here and now.

"Look, it won't be necessary. I'll call your father in the morning and make my apologies. You don't need me gate crashing your family's special day."

"Nonsense. You're coming." Connor strolled towards his office, loosening his tie before discarding it on the couch against the wall. "And speaking of special days, how come you never told me it was your birthday?"

He knew? "It's not important," Holly responded sharply.

"All birthdays are important. Besides, I got you something. Come in here for a minute."

Holly's heart hammered in her chest like a woodpecker at a tree trunk. *He'd bought her a gift?*

She placed her things carefully on her desk and stepped into his office. The door swung silently to a close behind her as he turned from his desk, a large cellophane-and-tissue-wrapped parcel in his hands.

"I noticed today how much you seem to like these things, but I wanted to get you something a bit different. Here, happy birthday."

Connor stepped forward and placed the white poinsettia in her hands. She didn't know whether to laugh or cry until weary emotion got the better of her and sudden tears sprang to her eyes. She blinked, hard, and kept her head tilted down, not trusting herself to speak. She would *not* break down in front of him.

"It's beautiful, Mr. Knight. Thank you."

"Hey, I thought we'd agreed you'd call me Connor." He lifted a long finger and tipped up her chin so she couldn't avoid drowning in the concern reflected on his face.

Her breath hitched, and she blinked again. Except this time she couldn't stem the acidic burn of moisture in her eyes.

"Tears, Holly?" His eyes narrowed as one fat tear hovered for a brief second then spilled off her lower lashes and tracked its inexorable path down her cheek to the corner of her lips. She turned her face, pulling away from the tenderness of his fingers, the pity in his gaze.

She'd had a lifetime of pity and she couldn't bear to look up and see more from him. Not now. Not ever. She swallowed against the lump in her throat, instinctively reaching for the anger she knew she needed to shore herself up and carry through with the rest of this farce.

"It's nothing. Just a headache, that's all." She held the gift with numb fingers, the crunch of the cellophane rippling in the air over her laboured breathing.

Connor stepped forward and removed the plant from her hands. "It doesn't look like nothing to me."

He put the plant back on his desk, then turned and caught her hands in his, drawing her closer until her breasts brushed against the fine-textured cloth of his suit. Beneath the fabric of her gown her nipples tingled and tightened almost painfully.

Her reaction to his nearness, to him, didn't go unnoticed. His eyes gleamed like black fire, his pupils dilating, almost consuming the rich dark brown of his irises.

For an infinitesimal moment Holly allowed herself to dream, to believe he might want her. To believe he might return her love. In that moment, she was certain, her heart laid itself bare to his scrutiny, her own eyes the shimmering window to her feelings.

But then the smouldering anger flamed back into life. Love, ha! He didn't love her. He pitied her. Otherwise why would she be here, pressed up against the hard wall of his chest, feeling the rise and fall of his breathing as it matched her own. She couldn't allow herself to be so vulnerable. Vulnerability was an indulgence she simply couldn't afford. She pulled free of his hold, her body mourning the loss of his heat even as she did so.

"I must go. Thank you for the plant." She wrenched the poinsettia back off his desk and swivelled on her heels to leave, silently castigating herself for a being a fool to want more than she had a right to.

Three weeks away from work, away from Connor Knight, would be a godsend right now. She wanted distance and she wanted it now. Yet a tiny chink in her rapidly assumed armour whispered, *Liar. You want him.*

"Holly—?" He caught her by her elbow and swung her around to face him.

Refusing to make eye contact, she stared blindly past his shoulder at the sparkling vista of the Auckland city lights, dazzling like a pirate's treasure against the skyline and inky black harbour beyond. He could keep his wretched pity and he could keep his blasted plant along with it.

He brushed another errant tear from her cheek with the back of his hand, his touch igniting the banked embers of desire she was working so hard to contain.

Contain it be damned.

She'd probably regret this in the morning. Heck, probably, nothing. Regrets were for the weak. If life had taught her anything it was how to be strong. To grab what you wanted and hold on tight. And right now, more than anything, she wanted Connor Knight.

The poinsettia dropped, unheeded, to the soft carpeted floor. The crinkle of cellophane as it rolled to one side, spilling a little dark soil on the pristine grey wool surface, barely registering against the roaring sound in her ears.

Holly reached up and laced her fingers at the back of Connor's neck and drew his head down to hers. She parted her lips, drawing in the taste of him before she pressed her mouth to his.

A jolt of shock shuddered through him. Shock and desire. Hot, hungry and hard. It had been years since he'd felt like this. Since he'd *allowed* himself to feel like this. Tonight Holly had struck at something deep within him. Something he'd held encased in ice, since desire and trust had been eviscerated from him by his ex-wife. Something that was now beginning to thaw.

Connor angled his head to taste her more deeply. While she'd led, he now took control. It was what he did best, and his body had been dormant for far too long. His tongue probed the moist recess of her willing mouth, stroking, tasting and wanting more. He slid his hands around to the small of her back, tilting her hips forward, drawing her closer towards his heat, his very need. A groan wrenched from deep in his throat at the contact—the warmth of her body igniting a fever in him, making him want with a savage hunger that ached through his entire frame.

He stroked one hand along the length of her exposed back, drawing her closer until he could feel the softness of her breasts pressing against his chest. And it wasn't enough. Right now, he felt like it would never be enough.

His hand travelled further, upwards to the nape of her neck, where tiny strands of fine dark hair had fanned out and escaped the confines of her formal hairdo. Tiny strands that had enticed and goaded him all evening to feel their soft-ness—a hint of the woman beneath the touch-me-not armour.

Her skin tightened and reacted to his touch, much as his had earlier this evening when she'd helped him transform into Santa Claus. But he felt anything but jolly and benevolent right now. He was like a dormant geyser, coerced into boiling, surging life. A geyser about to erupt.

His lips left her mouth. He had to taste her skin, to feel its texture against his lips, his tongue. He relished her sudden gasp as his tongue traced along the base of her hairline and he welcomed her weight as she sagged bodily against him.

Yet still, it wasn't enough, he wanted more of her. To touch. To see. To explore.

"Stay right where you are," he instructed, his voice nothing more than a husky growl.

Connor moved swiftly behind her and skimmed both hands under her dress to coax the fabric over her shoulders until with a 'shoosh' of lining it dropped forward. In the reflection of his privacy-tinted floor-length office window he watched, mesmerised as the falling fabric exposed the delicious line of her collarbone. The dim lighting of the office lent ethereal mystery and shadows to the creamy caramel of her skin.

"Lift your arms," he instructed, and slid the fabric down further as she did so.

A groan of approval, husky and raw, escaped him as he exposed the full roundness of her breasts, her dark rose-tinted nipples tight and distended.

"So beautiful," he murmured.

Holly felt a moment's panic as his warm breath sent flickers of dancing flame across the nape of her neck. She watched their reflection as his strong hands cupped her breasts, taking their weight, testing them. Then panic was overwhelmed by sensation as his thumbs stroked the aching peaks. Tension swamped her body, and her legs began to tremble as sensation arrowed to the core of her body, tighter and tighter until moist heat gathered then pooled in her panties.

She shivered and sucked in a breath as Connor nipped gently at the tender skin below her ear. The tiny pleasure-pain the pressure of his teeth left against her skin was foreign, yet deeply addictive at the same time.

She uttered a tightly strangled sob when his hands left her breasts. She wanted more with a desperation she'd never known. Not even when she'd been a child, wanting and needing a family to call her own. A family to belong to. She might not belong to Connor Knight forever, but she could belong to him for now—this moment—couldn't she? For this one exquisite moment?

She sighed as his hands trailed gently down her back to where her dress had arrested at her waist. The movement of his wrist was slight, but sufficient to send her gown cascading in a pool of crimson to her feet, exposing her matching lace bikini briefs and the length of her bare legs.

In the window she watched, mesmerised, as his hands slid over the gentle curve of her hips and the tension at the apex of her thighs ratcheted up another notch.

"Do you like what you see?" His voice was a tantalizing whisper in the shell of her ear.

Holly trembled as his hands slid around to the front of her body. One hand stroked upwards to caress her breast, and the other down where it slid inside the sheer lace of her panties and dragged them away to expose the dark coils of hair that led to her private core.

"Y-esss," the word hissed past her lips as he parted the folds of her flesh and gently stroked the centre of tension that wound her body hard against his like a bow. Unaccustomed sensation cascaded through her, building in undulating waves, but riding on the crest of those waves surfed a flicker of fear. She was losing control, surrendering absolutely to him.

"So do I."

His words were almost her undoing, yet she clenched her body tight—holding on, holding back, trying to regain some measure of restraint.

Connor slid one finger inside the liquid heat that threatened to send him over the edge. He struggled to meet the challenge of maintaining an intellectual distance from the vision in the glass and the waves of heat and passion that emanated from the woman shaking in his arms—against his insistent body.

Their reflection only served to incite him to a higher plane of need. Her glowing creamy skin fractured by the scanty line of red lace and framed by the darkness of his black suit behind her. The total contrast in their state of dress did nothing to lower the raging want that almost threatened to undo him, to send him uncontrollably over the edge in a way he hadn't experienced since his early teens.

He focused on Holly's face and noted, with powerful pleasure, how her eyes glittered. No longer with tears, but with a dark intense blue flame of passion.

With a slick finger he circled the hood of swollen flesh concealing the sensitive bud of nerve endings he knew would send her over the edge. Her breath quickened and the luscious swell of her breasts tightened and lifted as he gently increased pressure.

Her cry of release was a trophy to his ears, and he supported her body against the screaming responsive demands of his own as she shuddered to completion. He felt all-powerful. For the first time in forever, he felt like a man who had it all.

Well, not quite all, he acceded as he slid her underpants

further down, exposing the globes of her buttocks, buttocks that as they'd pressed against him had been driving him closer and closer to losing control.

He bent her forward, placing her hands to rest on the surface of his desk, and swiftly released himself from the confines of his trousers. He guided himself forward until his tip nestled at her entrance. He was acutely sensitive, still feeling the tiny tremors that pulsed through her, waiting, holding back until he could hold back no longer.

The guttural cry that ripped from his throat as he thrust forward was as foreign to him as the concept of making love to his PA on his desk, yet for some reason—here, now—it all seemed perfectly right.

She was tight, almost unbearably so, and from somewhere he miraculously found the strength to hold back until he felt her mould to his length, to sheath him with her wet heat until instinct overrode sensibility. Her body stiffened as he drove his full length into her and he reached around again to caress her sensitive nub. Taking the time to bring her to climax again was excruciating, until the rhythmic pull of her inner muscles took him suddenly, gloriously, over the edge.

Spent, mentally and physically, and breathing in great gulps, Connor collapsed over Holly's back. Bit by bit he became aware of their surroundings. Of the way his body pressed against hers, the feel of her silky smooth buttocks against his groin, her knotted fists beneath the spread of his fingers where he'd imprisoned them against the polished surface of his desk.

His desk.

The distant "ping" of the elevator returning to their floor rudely brought him to his senses. Someone was outside in the main office.

Reluctantly he withdrew from Holly and hastily rearranged his clothes before bending to assist her with the twisted swathe of her gown from where it lay about her feet.

As she slid her underpants back up, Connor caught sight of a telltale stain on her inner thighs. Blood?

"Here," he said, retrieving a handkerchief from his pocket, "You have your period."

"No." Her voice was strained. "It's not my period." She shimmied back into her gown, hiding the luminescent glory of her skin behind the rich glowing fabric.

"What?"

"I said I don't have my period." Holly smoothed her gown with shaking hands.

"You mean…" Connor was lost for words. *She was a virgin?* Or at least she had been until he'd taken her like a rutting stag. He grabbed her hand and stopped her as she started to walk away.

"Holly, you can't just leave. We need to talk."

A knock sounded at his inner office door.

"I think we've just said everything we needed to say for tonight." Holly lifted her chin and summoned every ounce of poise she'd worked so hard to develop. "Merry Christmas, Mr. Knight."

As an exit line she knew it was sadly lacking, but her mind was so scrambled she could barely think straight. She slid from his grasp and walked over to the door, swinging it open.

"Yes, Janet?" Holly dragged every scrap of composure she could garner. No mean feat when her heart still pounded like a marathon runner's and her legs were the consistency of jelly.

"I, um, I came upstairs to get my things, and I thought I heard something in Mr. Knight's office. I didn't realise you were still here." A flush of pink dusted the younger woman's cheeks, emphasizing the unsettled look in her eyes as her voice petered out. Holly only hoped her own embarrassment wasn't as visible.

Connor had drawn in behind her and stood like a shield at Holly's back. She stiffened at the sudden sense of heat and latent strength that emanated from him. A tiny quiver of pleasure rippled through her at the physical memory of his hard body behind her, within her, driving her past her prim and proper exterior and onto an entirely new level of living. She fought to control the urge to lean back against him and relive their lovemaking all over again.

"Is that all then, Janet?" Connor asked.

"Yes, sir."

"Then I think you should go, don't you?"

"Yes, sir."

"Merry Christmas, Janet."

"Merry Christmas to you too, sir, and you Holly."

"Thank you, Janet. Have a good holiday." Holly suppressed a hysterical bubble of laughter that rose in her throat. She couldn't believe how normal their exchange sounded. Inside, her heart was hammering a crazy tattoo, while on the exterior she felt like ice. She allowed herself a small sigh of relief when her assistant gave them both a weak smile and left them.

Alone, again.

Holly remained frozen where she was until rationality kicked in and she made for the door. She couldn't stop in case she threw herself at him again. Already she wanted more of him, more than she could ever ask for.

"Don't go. It's not over, Holly."

"Yes, it is. It has to be." With swift simple movements she gathered her garment bag and handbag and made it to the elevator before even taking another shaking breath. With each step she'd expected to hear Connor's footfall on the carpet behind her, yet when she stepped inside the elevator and turned to push the ground-floor button he remained silhouetted in the door to his office, his face inscrutable.

Behind him, his office appeared normal, unchanged—the clock on the wall giving evidence to the passage of but half an hour. Only half an hour? It felt like a whole new lifetime. Holly knew she would never feel normal again. But whatever happened after tonight, she would always be able to lock the memory deep within her to take out and examine and cherish at will.

The elevator doors took forever to close but finally they began to draw together. She bit back a cry of alarm as a dark-suited arm wedged between the closing elevator doors sent them springing wide apart again.

"What are you doing?" she asked, her voice high pitched and foreign to her ears.

"It may have escaped your notice but we didn't use protection. We need to talk. Besides which, that was your first time, Holly. For whatever reason, you chose me, and now I owe it to you to make tonight memorable and not just some denigrating experience."

Denigrating? He thought that had been denigrating?

"You don't need to—" Her protest was cut short by an implacable sweep of his hand.

"No, that's where you're completely wrong, Holly. I do need to. And, I will."

Four

Holly watched as Connor swiped his key card through the internal controls that permitted access to the penthouse apartment on the top floor of the tower that he used during the week when late nights didn't make it practical for him to fly back to his home on the island.

She knew she could stop him, if she really wanted to. He was nothing if not a gentleman. But she didn't want to. Not at all.

Despite the climate-controlled temperature in the elevator, a shiver ran down to the base of her spine. She'd only wanted to belong to someone for a moment, to have a connection, albeit fleeting. She hadn't dared dream for any more than that. From the time she'd been old enough to understand what had happened, that her mother was never coming back for her and there was no one else out there who cared enough to try and find her, Christmas Eve had always been the hardest day of the year.

It now struck her as ironic that despite all those years of conditioning, the one time she'd weakened and sought comfort had turned into her first sexual experience. A tug of heat reminded her that Connor had intimated there was more to come.

Was that why she hadn't put up any argument? Was she so pathetic that she'd take whatever he could hand out to her and be grateful? *Yes.*

Suddenly his comment about not using protection struck home. She'd acted purely on instinct, on basic need, and been so swept away by both the man and the moment that the possibility of pregnancy hadn't even occurred to her.

Stupid! Of anyone, she should have known better. There was no way she could have a baby. *No way.*

She silently counted back to the days of her last period. If all the overheard conversations in the staff cafeteria from the women desperate to become pregnant were any measure, she should be safe.

Well, there was always the morning-after pill. Provided, of course, she could find a dispensing pharmacy open on Christmas in the suburb where she lived. Yes, that's what she'd do. As soon as she could get back home she'd source the nearest one.

She stood to one side of the small enclosure as it raced to the top of the building, unsure about where this evening would end. For three years she'd been of no more interest to Connor than a fixture in his office, yet now he chose to spend the night with her? Her skin tingled—*the whole night?*

What had triggered this change in him? Carla! Of course, that was it. He'd been behaving out of sorts ever since his meeting with his ex-wife this evening. Anger and passion were both powerful, strong emotions. Holly knew, from her own tempestuous teenage years and the frustrated anger that had led her into so much trouble and seen her caseworker throw her hands up in surrender, how intrinsically mixed the two emotions could be.

So, he'd spent his anger on Carla, then he'd slaked his passion on her.

The realisation flayed her like a whip. Holly mentally squared her shoulders, absorbing the pain. She was a big girl, and well used to looking after herself. If he wanted to find comfort in her, so be it. They could each have their own agenda, fooling themselves for however long it took to burn out. And burn out it would, Holly had no doubt. On Connor's part at least.

For her, however, the physical act of love had only heightened her senses as far as he was concerned. The intimacy they'd shared in his office now made her more aware of him physically and emotionally.

And more in love with him than before.

The realization was as agonizing as it was hopeless. They were oil and water. The silver-spooned rich boy and the girl from the wrong side of town. The man who wanted children and the woman who swore she wouldn't.

Connor took her things as they stepped into the sumptuously furnished apartment and tossed them onto a leather-covered sofa. In silence he walked over to the bar and poured two glasses of wine before returning, like a panther on the prowl, to where she stood, waiting and unsure of what he expected.

He watched as she tilted the wineglass to her mouth and took a sip, his eyes drawn to the movement of her slender throat as she swallowed. He could still taste her, he realised. And he still wanted her with a fierceness that made his hand tremble slightly as he lifted his own glass in a silent toast.

"Could you become pregnant?" His stark question obviously startled her and she fought to regain her composure.

"That's impossible." She was emphatic.

"Nothing's impossible, Holly. What if it happens?"

She stared at him across the room, her eyes shooting sparks of blue fire. "I'm never having children."

Her words were like a knife twisting deep into his gut. They were harsh words from a woman her age and, ironically, words his treacherous ex-wife had never uttered, even though that had been her intention all along. The knife gave another sharp turn.

"So you're saying you'd terminate a pregnancy?" It was hard to keep anger from his voice, to maintain a rational, conversational tone.

"I didn't say anything of the kind. Don't put words into my mouth."

"Then what are you saying, Holly?" he demanded. "It might already be too late."

"If the worst did happen, I'd take care of it," she replied flatly.

"Take care of it," he repeated. "Why don't I get the impression you're discussing love and nurturing here."

"Look, I'm safe. I already told you that."

"So you say. Nothing's infallible, Holly. And I doubt you're on any form of contraception. Are you?" He gazed at her over the rim of his glass as she responded with a fierce shake of her head. Such fire, such passion. And all this over a conversation. What would she be like when she assumed that passion in the luxury of a large bed? There had been no denying her response to him earlier.

Heat, hot and heavy and clawing with need, engulfed his body.

One thing was for sure. Holly Christmas wouldn't be "taking care of it" if she was pregnant. Nothing would happen to another child of his ever again.

Grief tore at the ragged edges of his mind. He determinedly forced the crushing strength of the emotion aside. He'd take his time to grieve, later. The loss was still too new, too raw to even acknowledge. He needed to lock it away inside and deal with it on his own terms.

For now he intended to lose himself. To focus on the energy that seethed inside of him and turn it into something positive. Something that would surpass the loss and replace it with physical, pleasurable sensations.

Connor reached across and took her wineglass, placed it on a coffee table then reached to take her hand.

"I'd take care of you, Holly." It was a promise. If she carried his child he would ensure they both had the best of everything medicine and money had to offer.

"I can take care of myself." She lifted her chin in defiance of his words, yet her voice, tellingly, wavered. Her vulnerability cut him to the quick, and stark realization dawned. Take care of her? What the hell was he thinking? Had he been so addled by the intoxication of making love to her that he'd forgotten his position as her employer?

He forced himself to question his motives and, for the first time in forever, he didn't like the answers. Had he been so driven by the detestable evidence he'd been presented this morning that he'd subconsciously grasped at the next available opportunity? The thought was anathema to him, yet even so, he couldn't categorically state that in some dark and wounded corner of his heart he hadn't been provoked into manipulating the situation, manipulating Holly, to his own ends.

He dropped her hand as if her touch burned him. "Holly, I—" For the life of him he couldn't do it. He couldn't apologise for making love to her—especially when he wanted to do it again.

She lifted her hand and pressed her fingers gently to his mouth. "Shhh. Don't say it. Don't say you're sorry."

She knew him that well? Shock robbed him of speech, even more than the warm gentle imprint of her fingers against his lips.

"We're both adults," she continued, her voice slightly hesitant at first but growing stronger with each syllable. "We both know what we want. I'm not asking for forever, Connor. Just tonight. Only tonight."

Her fingers traced the outline of his lips and his body leapt to rock-hard attention at her touch. The sound of his name on her lips hung in the air, crashing through the final barrier of indecision. Intently he examined her face, her eyes, searching for the tiniest hint of reluctance, and could barely suppress his elation when he found none.

"Tonight, then." His throat felt raw as the words strained from him in agreement.

Sizzling anticipation shot scorching sparks through her. Her body felt taut, like a runner at the starting blocks, every nerve, every particle on alert. Waiting. Wanting.

"Ready?" Connor murmured as he lifted her hand to his lips and gently pressed them against her knuckles.

"Yes." Her voice was strong. There was no hesitation now. This was what she wanted. Her lips parted on a gasp of pleasure as his warm tongue stroked a hot, wet line between her fingers.

"Let's go, then."

In the softly lit bedroom he let her hand go. Holly stood on the threshold, seeing, but not really taking in, the lush draperies at the window and the hand-crafted armoire and matching dresser. Connor hit a switch on a remote and the curtains drew closed.

"Come here," Connor commanded from where he stood, next to the impossibly wide bed.

Shivering with nerves, Holly did as he bade.

"Undress me."

Where to start? Holly thought for a frantic second, then, almost of their own volition, her hands reached for the lapels of his jacket and pushed them wide, sliding the tailored garment off his broad shoulders and letting it drop to the floor.

She pulled his shirt free of his trousers and painstakingly undid each button from top to bottom until the fine white cotton hung free from his body. She reached for his hands, one at a time, and undid the cuffs on his sleeves, then pushed his shirt away to expose him to her.

He was beautiful. The latent strength of his body evident in the swell of his shoulders and the depth and breadth of his chest. She watched as a quiver ran over the taut muscles of his stomach, the same skin she'd barely grazed with her touch earlier tonight, yet could still feel searing her fingers.

She heard his swift intake of breath as she reached out and trailed her fingers across his belly before fumbling for the catch at his waistband.

"Stop." His voice was a deep-throated growl.

Her fingers halted their activity. Now she wanted to finish what she'd started. He knew already how painfully inexperienced she was, had he changed his mind?

"Touch me."

"Like this?" Her question was tentative. While she'd dreamed of touching him, the reality was hugely different. His skin tightened beneath her feather-light caress as she trailed her fingers over his chest and traced his nipples. To her surprise, and delight, they tightened into hard peaks, much like her own at this very minute. Did he ache for more, like she did?

With a groan, he grabbed her hands, halting them on their path as they trailed down past his belly button. "It's your turn."

"But—"

"But, nothing." He drew in a shuddering breath. "Undo your hair."

Holly lifted her shaking hands to slide out the pins that bound her hair, letting them scatter on the carpet at her feet and allowing the thick black swathe to uncoil and drape past her shoulders and down her back.

Connor ran his hands through the weighty length and she felt his fingers twist and curl in the tresses, gently tilting her head back. He lowered his head and captured her lips in a fierce sweep, demanding she surrender her mouth to him.

At first hesitantly, and then with increasingly more courage, Holly met his onslaught, giving as good as she got. Sucking at his tongue and swirling her own around his in a tango that turned her legs to water and her blood to molten lava.

She could feel how much he wanted her in the marble-hard lines of his body, and even though she knew it wasn't in the same way she wanted him, she would accept everything he had to give her. Her breasts ached to be touched, to be suckled as he suckled her tongue.

His hands skimmed down, pushing her dress over her waist to slide unhindered to the floor. The irony of how easily he'd undressed her wasn't lost, considering her inexperience in undressing him, yet she couldn't have cared less. She needed him holding her, touching her, inside her. Finally his lips were at her breast and a new tension built deep within her. A tension she was learning to identify. The rhythmic pull of his teeth and tongue over her sensitive nipples wrought a tiny scream of pleasure from her lips.

He swooped her off her feet, lifting her from her shoes and leaving a pool of clothing where she'd stood. She felt the fire of his skin as her breast pressed against his bare chest before

he placed her on top of the fine, cool sheets of his bed. There
had to be an acre of cotton, she thought wildly before she felt
the depression of his body next to her. The finely woven fabric
felt like a caress against her sensitised skin and even in the
dazed heat of passion its quality wasn't lost on her. She had
to hoard every memory, every sensation, and hold it fast to
her forever.

He'd removed his clothes, and the rasp of his legs along
her own made her squirm against the sheets. The hard dry heat
of his erection nudged her body, causing a deep-seated contraction to ripple wildly from her core—a prophecy of what
was yet to come.

"I won't hurt you this time, Holly," he whispered, his voice
laden with more promise than mere words could imply.

"But you didn't—" She stopped on a gasp as he traced her
lips with his tongue.

"Don't make me eat your words." A tiny smile played
around his lips as he nibbled across her jaw and over her neck.

The laugh that fought past the constriction in her throat surprised her. Humour, when she'd never felt more serious in all
her days? Life was full of contradictions.

She pressed against the bed as he gently licked and nipped
a line down her body, between her breasts, stopping to lave
at her belly button before dropping lower.

Propped as she was on a mound of pillows, the shadowed
view of his dark head against her skin made an erotic picture.
She could almost separate her mind from what was happening. Almost. But when she felt his warm breath against her,
through her panties, thought and reason fled on the building
waves of delight that undulated through her body.

She gripped wildly at the sheets, almost too afraid to draw
breath, as his tongue traced the leg line of her panties. His

fingers tugged the scrap of fabric away from her to be discarded onto the thickly carpeted floor.

Holly almost sprang off the bed when he replaced her panties with the hot wet pressure of his mouth. The surging waves of pleasure built and built inside, until she hovered so close to the brink of release she thought she might shatter.

His weight shifted just before she toppled over the edge, leaving her trembling, craving for more. He slid over her, stroking the line of her body with his hands. She felt him reach past her head and heard the tear of a foil packet. He held himself away from her momentarily and then he was nestling between her thighs. Hot, heavy and totally male.

"Open for me."

At his bidding she lifted her hips and let her legs fall open. He slid within her in one slick delicious movement. Her inner muscles tightened and released against the length of him as he pushed deeper until he was buried inside her. She luxuriated in the sensation of oneness with him, the deep sense of rightness in how they fit together. He'd had her heart for far longer than he knew, or would ever know, and now he had her body. She'd never felt drawn to another human being the way she was pulled to this man. Admitting how much she needed him both thrilled and terrified her. How would she cope when it was all over?

She sighed, the breath erratic, as he slowly withdrew before resettling back so deeply in her body she thought she'd pass out from the exquisite fullness of him. This was nothing like their first encounter where everything had been driven by the heat of the moment. This was making love on a completely different level. She could almost feel his heartbeat, hear his blood rush through his veins, breathe each breath he drew through his lungs.

Spirals of pleasure increased in intensity and urgency as he moved and she moved with him, sensually lifting to meet his every thrust, tilting away as he withdrew only to lift again to welcome his return.

The transition of time suspended, they were the only two people who existed. Locked in a cocoon of pleasure and need and, finally, satisfaction as they cleaved together in a joining that left them depleted yet still alive with exhilaration. Intimately locked together, Holly wrapped her arms about him as he rolled onto his side. She nestled against his chest, inhaling his male scent, committing it to memory as with a deep sense of sadness she remembered this could never last.

The persistent buzz of a telephone finally penetrated the fog that enveloped his brain. Who on earth would ring at such an hour? It couldn't be morning yet, Connor thought irritably as he attempted to roll over. Yet his mobility was impeded by a warm, lush body curved against him, by a swathe of black hair over his shoulders and by long silky legs entwined with his.

Gently he extricated himself and padded, naked, to where his suit jacket lay discarded on the plush navy carpet. He extracted his phone and flipped it open. He found the remote for the curtains and as they pulled open he stretched his back and noted the dull overcast sky.

Typical, he thought irritably. Another muggy, wet Christmas morning. *Christmas morning!* Remembrance dawned with sharp clarity just as his father's voice bellowed in his ear.

"Connor! You're on your way soon, yes?"

"Merry Christmas to you too, Papa."

"You're still bringing that secretary of yours?"

"Holly. Yes, I am. See you soon. *Ciao,* Papa."

He disconnected the call and looked across the room at the

enticing sleeping form draped across his bed. What a shame he couldn't take his time in waking her as he wanted, despite his body's instant reaction. He shook her bare shoulder gently, enjoying watching awareness dawn in her denim-blue eyes as he chased sleep away.

"Come on, my father is expecting us and we still need to stop by your place so you can change."

A wry smile twisted his lips as she shyly pulled the sheets about her, obscuring her breasts from view.

"Just give me a couple of minutes to gather my things." Her voice, husky and thickened with sleep, lit a flame within him he knew only one thing could extinguish.

"Shy?" He tugged persistently at the sheet until it fell away, exposing her. Already she was like a drug invading his senses. With damning clarity he knew one night with Holly would never be enough. So what if they were late, he decided as he pushed her back against the rumpled bedclothes.

They were running more than a little late when they drove out to her home so she could change into more suitable clothing. As they turned a corner into her street, Connor managed to hide his surprise when he saw the rundown housing area that Holly had reluctantly given as her address. Sure, in a few years, developers would be renovating the old state-built houses and making a killing, but right now that future seemed a million miles, and several million dollars, away.

"You can pull in here." She indicated a driveway on the cold, southern side of the road. Exposed as the dreary house was, it would get little natural sunlight through its tiny windows, he noted. He couldn't imagine why anyone would want to live like this. Certainly she could do better.

"How long have you owned this place?" he probed.

"I rent."

She *chose* to live here? Connor mentally reviewed the well-above-average sum he knew he paid her. Surely she could have rented somewhere more up-market. Or at the very least, he thought, as he cast a doubtful eye at the large party carrying on a few doors away where even at this hour patched gang members already spilled drunkenly onto the footpath, somewhere safer.

"I'll only be a minute."

"I'm coming in with you."

"Really, it's all right."

"Don't argue with me, Holly. You know you won't win."

Inside, the tiny house was no better. The fact she had to turn on the lights when it was only late morning spoke for itself. Naked bulbs in the ceiling fixtures cast stark light over meagre threadbare furniture. He tried not to curl his lip at the Formica-topped table and two vinyl-covered tubular steel-framed chairs standing askew on the cracked linoleum floor in the kitchen.

"Is this your furniture?" He couldn't help but ask.

"No, I rent the place furnished. Take a seat, and I'll get changed."

Not that it was any of his business, but what on earth did she do with her money?

"Don't I pay you enough?" The question dropped like a bomb in the room, and Holly halted in her tracks.

"You pay me very well." She held herself tightly coiled, as if she was hiding something and was afraid he'd find it. It was a side of her he'd never seen before, and he didn't like it.

"So what the hell do you do with it?" He swung out one arm, gesturing at the miserable conditions.

"Are you dissatisfied with the way I do my job?" Her voice was cold, yet vibrated with suppressed anger.

"Of course not. If I was, you'd know it."

"I'm glad that's settled, then. Because that's where we begin and end. What I do with my money is my business." With that she stalked from the room and into what he assumed was her bedroom. He could hear her moving about—slamming drawers, clattering coat hangers as if she had to vent her anger somehow.

She was right. He didn't like it one bit, but he had no right to push. There were ways and means of getting to the bottom of this. Connor shoved his hands deep into his trouser pockets and rocked on his heels, loath to sit on the sagging sofa positioned in front of the small television.

Through the paper-thin walls, the racket from the party down the street suddenly rose in volume and foul-mouthed jeers rang out through the air against the accompaniment of shattering glass bottles.

"Holly!" he shouted. "We need to go, now."

She reappeared in the doorway. She'd changed into smart pale-grey trousers with matching heeled sandals and a hot-pink short-sleeved blouse that lent a soft glow to her skin and served to detract from the faint shadows under her eyes. Shadows he himself had put there.

Connor urged her down the hallway. He guarded her back impatiently as she took the time to double lock and dead bolt the front door. Probably a total waste of time, he observed cynically, given the fact that it had glass panes that could easily be broken. He ushered her into the front seat of his 5-series BMW and pulled away from the driveway, the slight squeal of his tires as he planted the accelerator eliciting several one-fingered salutes from the partying throng.

Why did she live there, he asked himself again. Were there financial problems that necessitated it? Or some vice perhaps?

It occurred to him that he knew very little about her at all. But whatever secrets she was hiding, he would find them out.

Holly slammed her front door closed behind her and listened as the taxi sped away up the broken-glass-littered street. The day had been interminable. The polite smiles, the conjecture Connor's family couldn't quite hide from their eyes.

Certainly they'd been polite and friendly, his two brothers especially so. But all the while she felt as though she was being judged—and found wanting. Maybe they'd thought he'd bring someone more like Carla—social, outgoing and supremely confident.

She'd been a cuckoo in the nest. Again. The knowledge clutched like a fist around her heart. She should be used to that by now, yet the pain still had the power to bring her to her knees. Still, she was an old hand at hiding her pain deep inside, and that's where the memories of the past twenty-four hours would be firmly lodged.

Leaving hadn't been as difficult as she'd expected. In the end, she'd pleaded a headache to one of Connor's brothers and asked that he make Holly's apologies to everyone. For some stupid, foolish reason, she'd half expected to hear Connor come after her. Why, she didn't really know, because he'd been strategically monopolised by his father's other guests the whole time. He certainly hadn't noticed when she'd slipped from the front portico of Tony Knight's palatial Epsom home and into the waiting taxi she could ill afford.

Maybe he'd accepted that she didn't really belong. Or maybe he'd simply had his fill of her and made his point, whatever that was, with his father. She didn't know which hurt the most.

She dropped onto her bed, half the size of the one she'd slept in last night. The paradox was a joke—a bad one—and her hollow laugh echoed in the scantily furnished room. Deep down she had to admit that there was a tiny piece of her that still wanted the Cinderella finish—the knight in shining armour taking her to his castle to love her forever.

She gave herself a brisk mental shakedown. What had she been thinking? No, the sooner she put last night firmly in the past, where it belonged, the better. Difficult, though, when her body still hummed from the aftermath of Connor's lovemaking this morning and tiny twinges reminded her of the unaccustomed exercise she'd indulged in. And no matter which way she looked at it, it had been an indulgence. One she couldn't afford. After seeing him with his family, the close-knit group, the children, she'd realised with damning clarity that she'd never belong there. And nor could she when she was in no position to offer Connor what, she'd evidenced with her own observations today, he most wanted.

Children of his own.

Moping about the house wouldn't change anything, so Holly did what she did best—got on with things. First order of the afternoon was to find where the nearest urgent pharmacy was, then she'd call and see how Andrea was doing.

Bang, bang, bang! Holly all but leapt out her skin as a fist battered at her front door. Apprehensive, given the flavour of the neighbourhood, she peeped around her doorway and down the hall to the front door. An unmistakable figure loomed through the frosted glass panes.

"Holly, open up. I know you're in there."

She covered the distance to the door reluctantly, taking her time to unbolt the flimsy door and swing it open. He filled the open frame like a dark avenging angel.

"You left without saying goodbye." He stepped inside,

forcing her to flatten herself against the wall to avoid contact. Her shredded nerves couldn't take any more. "Are you okay?"

His hand lifted to her cheek. Holly flinched and pulled her head back. She couldn't bear it if he touched her again. She was strong, but not *that* strong. Challenge lit his gaze as his hand dropped down to his side.

"I'm fine. I thought it was better if I didn't make a fuss about leaving." Her heart pounded in her chest, and she took another step back. "Look. What we did last night was crazy. I was emotional because it was my birthday and you...well, I don't know why you wanted me, and I don't need to know. Let's not make life complicated by turning it into more than it was."

"And what was it, exactly?"

"We fulfilled a need, scratched an itch if you like. That's all."

"An itch?" His expression was deadpan, his voice level. Cool and calm, Connor Knight was formidable, and at this minute he scared Holly far more than if he'd developed a sudden rage at her words.

"For want of a better term, yes."

"What if I want more?"

"More?" her mouth dried and a bolt of desire shot with pulsing heat to radiate through her body. "There can be no *more*. It'll make working together impossible. People will talk...your father, you know his policy on office relationships." Frantic, Holly clutched at every reason she could—no easy feat with her mind just about fried from the dangerous heat in his coal-dark eyes.

"And that's it." His voice grew hard, cold.

"Yes. That's it. We're both adult enough to handle it, aren't we?"

Connor stood still as a statue. Bit by bit she saw a bleak coldness quench the fire in his gaze. His lips thinned in a tight line. A taut coil of tension emanated from him like a palpable thing. *Please, please, please,* she begged silently. *Just go!* Go before I change my mind. His jaw clenched and released as if he'd been on the verge of saying something then thought the better of it.

Down the hall her phone started to ring—the shrill sound grating through the atmosphere that hung thick between them.

A shiver of fear ran the length of her spine. The only calls she ever got were from Andrea's hospital. Something must be wrong for them to be calling now.

"I need to answer that. You can let yourself out." She turned to walk away but his arm snaked out to halt her in her tracks. He spun her back, and suddenly she was pressed against him, her body already willingly forming to the hard lines of his.

"Just one more thing," he growled.

Connor pinned her against the wall, pressing his lips against hers in a hard, possessive move that left her in no doubt of his anger. She pushed the flats of her hands against the wall behind her to stop herself from reaching out to touch him. Yet, despite her best intentions, she couldn't help but respond to the commanding sweep of his tongue, and her lips parted in reluctant welcome.

The instant she surrendered, he broke away and turned to stalk down the cracked, uneven concrete path. Away from her house and away from her. Holly could only watch, helpless yet thankful he'd done so before she threw herself back at him, plastered herself against his body and begged him to stay.

Five

At the private convalescent hospital nestled quietly in vast lawns on the northern-facing slopes of one of Auckland's prestigious suburbs, Holly brushed her foster sister's fine hair against her pillow. It was the only thing to soothe Andrea today.

"Sorry to have disturbed your Christmas," the nurse at the foot of the bed remarked. "She just seemed worse today. We tried earlier to get a hold of you to let you know."

"I know. I'm sorry," Holly answered with a worried smile. "You did the right thing to call me in."

"I hope we didn't interrupt anything important."

"No," she managed through stiffened lips, "nothing that couldn't be left."

"Maybe next Christmas there'll be someone special to sweep you off your feet," the nurse continued with a wink. "You never know just what's around the corner."

Heat suffused Holly's cheeks. No, you never did know

what was around the corner and that was precisely why she was never sleeping with Connor Knight again. The nurse didn't know quite how close she'd struck to the bone. Holly smiled a brief response and put the hairbrush down, looking at Andrea's tragically uncommunicative twitching form in the bed. She was a far cry from the exuberant adolescent who'd egged her on to believe in herself when no one else would. Fate had finally smiled on them both when they'd been placed in a home together.

While it was highly unlikely Holly carried the juvenile Huntington's gene that slowly and painstakingly stole her dearest and closest friend from her, who knew what time bomb she could pass onto her children? And for as long as Holly was responsible for paying for Andrea's care, she couldn't afford the investigators necessary to try and trace her own parents.

So it was simple. No children. Ever. Andrea was far more important than anything else right now. Including Connor Knight.

Back at work just over a month later, Holly was grateful she'd had no other demands on her time. Andrea's deterioration over the break had been marked, and Holly had been forced to request to use up the balance of her accrued leave so she could spend every available minute with her. It had taken some juggling, but Janet had happily returned early from her holidays to fill in.

The emotional demands of remaining positive for Andrea had left Holly totally wrung out by the end of each day, and now the onset of a mild yet persistent tummy bug meant that she'd have to restrict her visits until she was better again. At first she'd panicked, terrified she was pregnant, but the light period she'd had two weeks ago made that impossible. Thank God.

Holly's feet dragged as she stepped down the corridor to her office. The poinsettias hadn't suffered for the lack of natural light at her workstation, she observed ruefully. Obviously, someone had kept them watered during her extended break, although they did seem a bit washed out for colour. How symbolic, she thought, cynicism twisting her lips, just like her.

She'd lost weight and her appetite had been reduced to nil. How she'd contracted this wretched stomach bug was beyond her, although she had her suspicions about the efficiency of her ancient refrigerator, with its damaged door seal, combined with Auckland's high summer humidity. The mix was bound to have wreaked havoc on the food she'd managed to force past her lips.

In response to the thought of food, her stomach heaved slightly. Holly took a deep levelling breath and waited for the nausea to subside.

The white poinsettia was nowhere to be seen. She supposed the cleaners must have disposed of it when they'd cleaned up the mess it had left after landing ignominiously on the carpet on Christmas Eve. That night seemed so long ago.

She hadn't heard from Connor. He'd been away at his family's holiday home on the Coromandel Peninsula during the two weeks immediately after Christmas, and HR had handled her request for additional time off in his absence. Even if he had tried to call her once he was back in Auckland, she'd been at the hospital most of the time, only going home to sleep late at night, then racing off early to catch the succession of buses that took her back to Andrea. Besides, it was exactly what she'd wanted. No fuss, no complications and certainly no recriminations to interfere with her ability to do her job and earn her desperately needed income.

"Good morning, Holly."

Connor stood in the doorway to his office. It was all she could do not to jump at the sound of his voice. She hadn't allowed herself to realise, until now, how much she'd missed the timbre of her name on his lips. How much she'd missed *him*.

"Good morning, Mr. Knight."

Holly busied herself putting her handbag away and checking the papers in the in-box on the corner of her desk. She heard Connor sigh from behind her.

"I think we've gone past you calling me Mr. Knight, don't you?"

"Yes, sir. We did. But that was last year."

"So we're to pretend it never happened?" Was it her imagination or had the liquid velvet in his tone suddenly turned to molten steel?

"I had a wonderful birthday. Thank you." She kept her head averted. There was no way she could meet his gaze. He'd see too much. He'd see how much she loved him, how much his lovemaking had meant to her. She couldn't do that. Not now, not ever.

She would never be a part of his world, just as he could never understand hers. She'd learned that particular lesson when she'd been placed in a home more affluent than most. A budding adolescent already with the attitude from hell, she'd appealed just a little too much to the teenage son of her caregivers. They hadn't believed her claims when she'd finally drummed up the courage to tell her new foster mother of his unwelcome attentions. They'd closed ranks, snapping together like a gilded trap, telling her caseworker that her behaviour was uncouth at best and that she'd never fit in. Perhaps she'd be more comfortable with a different family. One on the other side of town. Holly had learned that "like stuck with like."

Pushing back the pain of past hurts, Holly jerked her mind

back to the present. Andrea needed her now, more than ever before. A relationship with Connor Knight was a luxury she couldn't afford.

Her phone rang and she lifted the receiver. "Connor Knight's office, Holly speaking."

"Holly, it's Miriam Sanders."

The administrator at Andrea's hospital. Icy-cold fear shrouded Holly's body. Her fingers gripped the phone, squeezing so tight it hurt. "Yes?"

"Look, this is difficult for me to say, but Andrea's needs have been reassessed in light of her recent deterioration, and I'm afraid we've had to revise the cost of her care."

Holly slumped in relief issuing a silent prayer of thanks it wasn't the news she'd been dreading.

"How much more?" She held her breath. When the administrator mentioned the sum it was all she could do not to scream "No!" into the receiver.

"So as you can see," the woman continued, "we need your guarantee of payment."

Holly did a quick mental calculation. With a bit more juggling she could meet the increase, just. "Yes, I'll pay. I'll find the money from somewhere." She hung up the telephone with a wrenching sigh.

"Problem?" Connor's voice made her jump. She'd forgotten he was there. Listening. How much had he heard?

"Nothing I can't handle." Her stomach pitched again uncomfortably, and she blindly started to sort through the mail on her desk, willing him to turn away and go back into his office. Willing him, against everything her mind and her body cried out for, to just leave her alone.

The almost silent swish of his door closing gave her the answer she sought, yet cut her to the quick. Stop being an idiot, she rebuked silently. What did you expect? That he'd sweep you in his arms and tell you he'd make everything all right? That he loved you? Ha! Not in this lifetime.

The printed words on the correspondence she gripped tightly between her fingers shimmered and swirled. Holly blinked back the tears that threatened to fall. Since Andrea's condition had declined so severely her emotions had been such a mess.

The day passed in a blur. A blur peppered by Janet's excitedly related story about how she had met some wonderful holiday squeeze at New Year. Holly tried to summon the energy to be happy for her, but failed miserably. Instead, she struggled to focus on the work at hand—a particularly sensitive contract that Connor had dictated specific alterations to.

She worked long into the evening on the document, heedful that Knight Enterprises expected to close this deal with a major public fanfare and had courted both print and television media for some time about releasing the details. Her head and neck ached with the strain of sitting at her computer station without a break. While Janet had brought her several cups of tea during the day, more often than not they'd cooled in the mug unnoticed as her fingers continued to fly over the keyboard.

"Here you are, Miss Christmas. I know you've hardly taken a break today so I thought you might need something to eat."

Holly lifted her attention from the bundle of papers on her desk to smile her thanks to Janet. Her words hovered precariously at the edge of her lips as the smoked mussel salad, a specialty from the restaurant in the complex at the base of the tower and enticingly presented on the boardroom's best china, sent her stomach on a sudden looping roller-coaster ride.

"How thoughtful. Thank you, Janet." She managed, swallowing against the nauseating metallic taste that flooded her mouth. She hastily averted her eyes. "Will you excuse me? I think I need to freshen up a bit first."

"Are you okay? You've gone awfully pale."

"Yes—yes. I'm fine. I'll be back in a minute." Her ears roared, and the back of her neck felt as though it was encased in a cold, clammy grip as she forced the words past her lips and swept around the side of her desk.

Stay down, stay down, stay down. She said the words over and over in her mind, praying the silent mantra would help her maintain her equilibrium until she made it to the ladies' room.

Thankfully the stalls were all empty, and Holly slammed and locked the door behind her and dropped to her knees, her hands clutching the cold porcelain as if her life depended on it while she dry-retched over the bowl.

With watering eyes and shaky hands, she tore off a few squares of toilet paper and wiped at her face. When would this end? She'd have to see a doctor soon. If she didn't get on top of things, she couldn't visit Andrea, and as much as she'd wanted to deny the specialist's report and ignore the sorrow in his eyes as he'd delivered the latest news, she knew she wouldn't have her precious friend much longer.

Holly's chest tightened painfully at the admission before she resolutely pushed the thought aside. She couldn't deal with that now. Some things were just too much to bear. She hauled herself upright and leaned back against the door while she waited for the dizziness to subside, which finally, thankfully, it did.

Janet had returned to her own desk by the time Holly re-emerged on the scene. Without looking too closely at the contents of the plate, she lifted it from her desk and took it to the kitchenette off their office suite, hastily dumping the contents in the plastic-lined bin and throwing a few paper towels over the top for good measure.

She settled herself back at her desk, trying to make sense of the scattered words on her screen.

Connor came out of his office and leaned against her desk. "Are you okay? Janet said you weren't looking too well a minute ago."

"She's exaggerating, really. I'll be fine."

"Whatever, it's time you called it a day. You look shattered."

"The contract's almost complete. If you're sure you don't need me…?" The words she'd left unspoken trailed away into nothing at the fire that blazed dark and hungry in eyes that all day had been as cold and glittering hard as obsidian.

"Need you, Holly?" Cynicism curled his lips, and she futilely wished her words unsaid.

"Right, I'll be off then." She severed eye contact, hastily gathered up her things and switched her monitor off.

"Before you go, come into my office." He didn't wait for a response.

All the remaining energy she had left within her sagged from her body in a whoosh. Holly steadied herself against her desk struggling to summon the reserves she needed to face him again.

"Yes?" she enquired as she hovered in the doorway.

"Come in and close the door."

Her nerves jangled as she did as instructed and came further into his office. She averted her eyes from his desk and the view beyond it. Holly didn't think she'd ever be able to walk in here again and not see the two of them, their reflections as starkly painted in her mind's eye as they'd been in the glass reflection that night only a few weeks ago.

"Take a seat," Connor instructed firmly.

"I'd prefer to stand. This will only take a minute, won't it?"

"That all depends," he answered.

"Depends? On what?" Holly clenched the straps of her handbag so tight her fingers hurt.

Connor came closer and took her by the elbow, leading her firmly to the long sofa at the end of his office. "Sit."

She sat, perched at the edge, and pulled her legs away slightly as Connor loomed over her.

Holly looked about as frightened as a deer caught in a hunter's sights, Connor realised. What was she hiding? He'd tried several times during her holiday to contact her, but she didn't answer her phone at home and when he'd driven by she hadn't come to the door.

There was nothing for it but to cut straight to the chase, he decided. "Why are you sick?"

"What?"

"Are you pregnant?"

"No!" Holly shot to her feet and swayed slightly, her face bleached white at the sudden movement.

Connor pushed her back down in the chair and lowered himself next to her. He could see her pulse fluttering in her neck, like a trapped bird, against the alabaster of her skin.

Most people came back from their summer holiday tanned and rested. Holly's skin, usually filled with a warm glow that had nothing to do with sunshine was now wan and sallow, and unhealthy shadows underscored her eyes.

"Are you sure? You've seen a doctor?"

"Of course I'm sure. I would never make a mistake about something like that. *Never!*"

Her vehement response took him aback. He rose from the couch and went to pour a glass of water from the cut-crystal carafe on the antique sideboard against the wall. Their fingers brushed as he handed it to her, sending a surge blazing up his arm. The weeks apart hadn't dulled the edge of his hunger for her. If anything, the aching need to be with her again was even stronger.

"What's wrong then?" he pressed. "You haven't been sick once in the three years you've worked for me."

"Something I ate this week hasn't agreed with me. That's all."

"You've been sick for a week?"

"I've only been feeling a bit off colour for a day or two. I'm sure it'll pass soon."

"Take tomorrow off."

"That's quite unnecessary, it's just a mild tummy bug. Now, if that's all you wanted me for…?" Holly stood, more slowly than before, and walked towards the door. There was no legitimate reason he could keep her here any longer.

"Have dinner with me."

She stopped and turned. "I beg your pardon?"

The words had sprung from his mouth before he'd had time to consider them fully, but now he'd had a second or two to turn the idea over in his mind it sounded like a good one.

He rose and walked over to her. "Have dinner with me. I know you've barely eaten all day and you must be starving. Just something simple, okay?"

Holly's stomach growled in response. She grimaced and placed a hand over her abdomen, a movement that caught Connor's eye. Quickly she let her arm drop. It wouldn't do to give him any further ridiculous ideas.

"I should get going, I'll miss my bus."

"Damn it, Holly. I'll take you home. What kind of man do you think I am? I'm not asking you to leap into bed with me!" Although the prospect of doing just that painted a vivid image of the two of them—naked, together—with such sharp clarity his entire body tensed. He held his breath waiting for her to reply. Her determinedly obvious inaccessibility had made him begin to question why it was so important to him that she say yes. All he knew was since that night, here in his office and upstairs in his bed, he'd wanted more of her in every way. It wasn't enough to have her working at her desk outside his office. He wanted her by his side. In his bed.

"Yes, all right."

Just like that? He had to put his libido on hold and double take on what she had agreed to. With unaccustomed sluggishness his brain finally caught up and overcame the raw desire that surged with a seething hunger.

"Great. Let's go, then."

Traffic was light along the Auckland waterfront at this time of the evening. Hundreds of walkers, joggers and families on their bikes were still out enjoying the warm summer evening despite the encroaching night. Connor pulled his car into a car park that fronted onto the beach at Mission Bay.

"Let's take a walk along the beach before we have dinner," he suggested, and took Holly's hand, guiding her towards the promenade.

It was a gorgeous evening. The last of the sun's rays spread in a flash of darkest red through to the palest orange. The light reflected across the gentle sea in the harbour. Seagulls wheeled and dived through the air, shrieking their strident cry as they scouted out for the nearest scrap of food. Mission Bay was easy pickings for any bird, including the fat pigeons that cooed and strutted along the path by the sea wall.

Bit by bit Holly began to relax and started to feel a lot better. The fresh air and gentle exercise seemed to be doing her good, and her appetite had quadrupled by the time they'd meandered past the massive fountain at the centre of the domain and crossed the main road towards the plethora of restaurants on the other side.

"How do you feel about Italian? If you'd prefer, we can take a table on the pavement."

"That'd be great, thank you." Without realizing it, he'd given her the perfect opportunity to avoid the aromas that permeated the interior of the restaurant. Outside, the light breeze would ensure her sensitive stomach didn't overreact.

Either they were extremely lucky, or Connor Knight had a way with the maître d' because miraculously, and despite being very busy, a table for two was available.

"White wine or red?" Connor asked as he perused the wine list.

Her taste buds soured at the thought of drinking wine. "I'll stick with water tonight."

"Good idea. Me too. We'll have two of these." He pointed to the New Zealand branded bottled spring water on the list and handed it back to the waiter.

"So, do you come here often?" Holly broke the silence that had settled between them.

Connor laughed, the spontaneous sound lighting a warm ember deep inside her chest. "I think that's supposed to be my line."

Holly smiled weakly in response. Okay, as conversation starters went it had been a bit weak, but there was no rule book to cover polite conversation with your boss over a late dinner—especially when one heated look from him was enough to set up a chain reaction inside her that had nothing to do with pain. Except, perhaps, the pain of denial.

Connor continued, "It's been a while since I've been here, but the food's always been very good. What do you feel like?" He flicked a glance at her over the top of his menu.

You. Holly suddenly put her fingers over her mouth. Oh, God, she hadn't said that aloud had she?

"The fish looks good. If your stomach's still a bit weak you might find that light enough."

She heaved a sigh of relief. "Yes, that sounds great. I'll have the poached terakihi and a salad."

The waiter rematerialised to take their orders, Connor placed her order and chose scaloppini for himself.

"You used to work in the typing pool, right?" His question, out of the blue, startled her.

"Yes," she replied cautiously.

"You were such an earnest young thing."

Surprised he'd even noticed her back then, Holly just nodded. Connor stroked the condensation from the side of his glass with one long finger. She couldn't tear her eyes away from the movement, nor bring herself to take a sip of her water to relieve her suddenly very dry throat.

"What made you decide to become a PA? I would've thought you'd have gone for a degree at the university. Law, maybe."

As idly curious as his comment was, all Holly's shutters came racing down. She'd held her cards so close to her chest for so long now it had become second nature. If you shared nothing, you couldn't lay yourself open to ridicule or worse, pity. While part of her ached to tell Connor more about her past, the lines, as she knew them, had been clearly delineated many years ago. In life there were the "haves" and the "have nots." Those lines weren't made to be crossed.

"I thought about it," she admitted, pushing a piece of fish around her plate with her fork, "but I decided I'd rather get my teeth into a job where I could start earning straightaway."

She would have given anything to complete a degree at Auckland University, but in her world there had been no well-heeled parents to supplement a student loan. If she was to get anywhere in life it would be on her own, just like she'd been since the day her mother had left her.

"Money's that important to you you'd give up doing something you really wanted?"

Holly's throat closed. Something she really wanted? All her plans—*what she'd wanted*—to save enough money to start an investigation into who she really was and where she'd come from—had come unstuck with the onset of the latter stages of Andrea's illness when Holly had assumed responsibility for the financial maintenance of Andrea's care. She owed it to her foster sister, and more. Andrea had been the one person who'd stuck up for her and who'd forced her to take a long hard look at what had become self-destructive behaviour. She owed her foster sister her very existence. Looking after Andrea, for however much longer she lived, was something Holly was bound by both love and honour to do.

"You can't deny that money is important. Look at your own family." She attempted to deflect his attention from herself. "I've heard the stories about how hard your dad worked when you were just a boy. You don't build a corporation like Knights without a lot of hard work. He never had any degree."

"True. But it came at a far bigger cost than just money. He was a stranger to us while we were growing up. When our mother died, it was like he'd died, too, for all we saw him. Believe me, Holly, money isn't everything."

"And so says the man who has everything." Holly couldn't stop the bitter words from escaping her mouth and desperately wished them unsaid when she saw his face. His eyes glittered darkly and his lips settled in a straight line.

"Not everything, Holly. Some things you can't buy."

"I'm sorry, I shouldn't have said that."

"Come on, it's getting late and you look like you've done about ten rounds in the boxing ring. I'll take you home."

Six

Connor stared out the window of his penthouse apartment, watching as the world hurtled by regardless of the late hour. Try as he might, he couldn't get Holly out of his mind. What was it with him and women that it always came down to money? She'd made no bones about how important money was to her, yet, if that was the case, why did she live where and how she did? She was a conundrum. One he had every intention of figuring out even though logic told him he should just forget their night together, as she had so conveniently managed to do.

Logic could take a hike.

He turned from the window and flipped open his cell. One press of a quick-dial would take him a step closer to the answers he needed.

The summarised report, when it came through to his private fax line in the morning, did little to calm his disquiet. It was clear Holly had major financial issues, not least of which were large sums of money being paid out on a very regular basis—most of her wages in fact. No wonder she lived in such squalid conditions. Something, or someone, drained every dollar she earned. The only savings account she'd had was well in the past, and it had been cleared out completely several months ago. But all the financial information aside, the report did nothing to shed any light on exactly *who* she was.

The memory of the conversation he'd overhead between Holly and another person yesterday tickled at the back of his mind. She had financial pressure from somewhere, but where? Was it gambling, or worse?

He called his private investigator again.

"I need you to go deeper. Find out who she is, where she's from. Everything. I don't care how long it takes."

Holly let herself into the house and locked the door behind her before making her way to the bathroom. The past week had been interminable. Wearying queasiness still plagued her and kept her from visiting Andrea. While the staff at the hospital understood, it didn't help assuage the guilt she felt at not being able to be there herself.

To make matters worse, not only had she been sick at work again but this time Janet had seen her and had been full of overwhelming fuss. To gain some respite, Holly had agreed to Janet's suggestion that she should go home for the day. Connor was tied up in a video conference call when she'd gathered her things and headed for the door. The last thing she'd needed had been his concern, as well.

As she'd searched for change for the bus in the bottom of her bag she'd come across the emergency sanitary items she kept in a small cosmetic purse. Connor's question from last week rung hollowly in her ears. She'd been adamant at the time that she couldn't be pregnant, but could she? Really? She couldn't hide from the possibility any longer.

Holly put the pharmacy packet she'd brought home onto the vanity of her tiny bathroom and removed its contents. The instructions were simple. Too simple really, when it was something so terrifyingly important. She followed the steps to the letter, then paced the tiny confines of room like a caged animal, an analogy that rang a little too close to the truth for her comfort.

She forced herself to calm down, to take stock of the situation. To breathe. And started to pace again. Her mind whirled in ever-diminishing circles—bringing her back to the same conclusion every time.

She couldn't be pregnant. She just couldn't. Life couldn't be so unfair as to twist its jagged blade into her so cruelly. Not with so many questions unanswered and certainly not in her current financial position. Never in her worst nightmares had she ever imagined this happening to her. She'd promised herself never to have a baby until she knew she wouldn't be bringing ill health and unhappiness to another life and, even then, only if she could provide it with the things she'd never had—a background, the unconditional love of two parents and the financial security to meet all its needs.

The sound of a car pulling up outside her house brought her pacing to an abrupt halt. There was only one person it could be. A bolt of queasiness hurtled from her stomach. She swallowed against it and willed her body back under control.

Footsteps echoed on the path—pounding inexorably closer to her front door. A heavy knock made the flimsy door rattle angrily inside its frame. Holly dragged a steadying breath through tightened lips.

"Holly!" Connor Knight shouted through the glass.

Her legs trembled as she walked down the short narrow hall and cautiously opened the front door the scant few inches the security chain allowed.

"Let me in, Holly." His voice was liquid velvet, soft and sensual and spoke to her on a physical level that made her heart leap skittishly in her chest, yet despite the virtual stroke against her psyche there was an underlying steel in his tone that demanded he be obeyed.

Holly took a small step back. "No."

"Open the door." His voice grew louder.

"You can say what you need to from where you are and leave."

"Janet said you were sick—again. Don't think you can fob me off this time, Holly." He bit the words out, and they ricocheted around the barren front porch.

A young boy riding past on his skateboard, stopped on the sidewalk. "Hey, miss, you wan' me to go get my uncle? He'll get rid of the suit for ya!"

Holly recognised the boy from the house a couple of doors away, and she had no doubt that one of his many "uncles" had been members of the throng that had partied hard on Christmas Day.

"Holly?" Connor stared at her through the gap, his brows pulled together in a forbidding line. "Would you like the young man to get his uncle? Go ahead, I'm in the mood."

She swallowed against the lump in her throat and raised shaking fingers to the door, closing it enough to slide the chain back off then pulling it wide open.

"It's okay. I know him." She gave a weak smile over Connor's broad-suited shoulder and watched as the boy gave a cheeky grin before boarding further down the street. "You'd better come in." She gestured to Connor to follow her down the narrow hall.

"Thank you."

Who'd have thought two simple words could have been laced with such fury? For a minute she wondered if she'd done the right thing. Maybe having one of the heavies from up the street "take care of him" for her might not have been such a stupid idea after all. Holly discarded the thought immediately. No. She had to face this, as she'd had to face every crossroads in her life. Somehow, she'd make it.

"Can I get you coffee or tea? I'm sorry I don't have milk, though." The fridge had totally given up the ghost during the night, and Holly had tipped out the gelatinous remains of her milk before heading to work in the morning.

"No. I don't want anything except a few honest answers."

"I've never been anything but honest with you," Holly retorted, stung at the implication.

He pushed his hands in his pockets and looked around the room. "That's good. So there's no need to stop now, is there?"

What on earth was he getting at? Did he know about the pregnancy test? Holly didn't have to wait long to find out.

"When Janet told me you'd been sick, I thought you might prefer a ride home rather than catch the bus. I sent her after you this afternoon when you left. I was surprised to hear you took a little shopping detour before going to the station." He removed his hands from his pockets and caught her upper arms, his fingers tightening slightly. "So have you taken the test yet, Holly? Were you going to tell me the result?"

She tried to twist free, but he held her firm. The heat of his fingers imprinted on her skin and, damn it, she couldn't help but want to feel them touching other parts of her. She was nuts. Only a crazy woman reacted this way with so much at stake.

"I can't believe you made her spy on me." She turned her head so he couldn't see the flare of desire she knew reflected in her face. "Let me go."

"Tell me." The demand was no less forceful than the glare in his eyes.

"I don't know."

"Which—the result, or if you'd tell me?"

"Neither! Both! I…I don't know!" Holly wrenched herself loose from his intoxicating hold. "I was taking the test when you arrived."

"Where is it?" He demanded.

"On the bathroom vanity," Holly replied in a tiny voice, frozen to the spot, as he strode past her, headed straight for the bathroom.

His footsteps halted in the bathroom, and her stomach clenched as she waited. A sound, like a muffled groan, filtered through the hallway, then silence. Eventually she heard the pipes clank in protest and water run in the basin. One look at his face and his slightly reddened eyes when he returned, and Holly's world tilted sharply. Disoriented, she grabbed the back of one of the tubular steel chairs Connor had eschewed so disdainfully during his last visit.

"No!" The wail broke from her throat. "Tell me it isn't true!"

Cold fury glistened in his eyes. "Oh, it's true all right. You're pregnant with my child."

Another wave of nausea, more persistent than before, rose with a surge of determination she couldn't disregard.

"Oh, God!" With her hand clamped to her mouth, Holly made short work of the distance to her bathroom.

Spent with exhaustion a few minutes later, she dimly became aware of Connor's presence behind her, of his strong, warm hand gently stroking her back. Tremors of shock rippled through her as she leaned weakly against the porcelain, the hard floor pressing against her knees.

"You all done?" He sounded distant, emotionally removed.

"I think so."

"Then wash your face and come with me."

"Come with you?" Holly was confused. "Back to work?"

Connor offered his hand and helped her to her feet, a line of tension between his brows as he turned the taps on at the stained basin. Holly grabbed a flannel and dashed it under the trickle, scrubbing at her face before scooping up some water with her hand to rinse her mouth. Connor handed her a towel and stood silent as a statue while she mopped her face dry.

"No. To a doctor."

Seven

"She's pregnant, early days, but definite."

Connor looked up at the softly spoken words as the doctor, one of his female cousins, closed the door to her examination room behind her allowing Holly some privacy to get dressed.

"Hell." Connor stopped his pacing and dropped into the seat across from Carmen's desk.

"She's the one you brought to Christmas brunch, isn't she?" Connor nodded.

"I thought Uncle Tony had strict rules about office romance."

"It was an aberration."

"Unprotected sex is some aberration."

"She assured me she was okay." Connor couldn't meet her gaze, or read the reproach he knew would be there.

"Well, looks like you have some rethinking to do, cuz."

"Yeah." More than Carmen could ever realise. Connor flung a look at the still-closed door. "Will she be okay?"

"Once she starts to eat properly and gets plenty of rest. I'll give you a list of supplements to help build her strength up. She hasn't been looking after herself that well. If you two are going to have a healthy baby, that has to change."

A healthy baby. Connor's head spun. *He was going to be a father!* Moisture sprang to his eyes. He blinked it away as emotion cascaded through him, tightening his chest and setting a fire of hope burning low in his gut.

"Don't worry, I'll make sure she takes care of herself."

Holly remained on the examining table, the doctor's parting words still ringing in her ears. "No doubt you and Connor will need to talk."

Holly couldn't even acknowledge her. Her hand slid to her lower belly and pressed against the flat surface. Disbelief raged through her mind. Pregnant.

In all her worst nightmares she'd never imagined this could happen. Not to her. Never to her. She'd always been so careful never to let anyone close enough. The one time in her life she'd let go of reason and given in to impulse, to admit to the need for another—a need she'd guarded against for so long—and fate threw this savage twist at her.

Holly shuddered. She couldn't afford to bring up a child. She could barely afford to support Andrea, let alone herself. The financial demands of a baby didn't bear thinking about. She drew her knees up and curled into a protective ball. What the hell was she going to do?

Holly's heart twisted sharply in her chest. If she'd had the luxury of normal circumstances, the news would have sent the blood in her veins singing with joy to know she carried Connor's child, yet the fearful weight of responsibility paralysed her. What if there was something wrong? She couldn't bear to watch another person she loved die a slow and painful death.

Her breath caught in her throat. Love? She couldn't love the baby already. It was far too soon. In fact, never would be too soon. Holly pulled down the shutters on her emotions. She couldn't afford to feel anything for this new life growing inside her. Not when there was so much at stake.

Slowly she uncurled and pushed away the sheet the doctor had draped over her for privacy. *Privacy*—the term was completely incongruous after an internal examination.

The muted murmur of voices filtered through the door. She had to get moving. She didn't put it past Connor to be making plans with the doctor. Plans *she* should be making.

At least this meant she wouldn't have to restrict her visits to Andrea because of her assumed stomach flu. The weighty responsibility of another life rocked her again. *What on earth was she going to do?*

The door across the room opened.

"You okay?" Connor asked, his lips a grim line, and expectation shining in his eyes she couldn't quite identify.

The strangled sound that dragged itself from her throat could have passed for a laugh any other day of the week but failed miserably right now. "Okay? No. I'm not okay. I couldn't be worse." She couldn't hold back the bitterness from her words, nor did she want to. She wanted to run from the room, from Connor. From the truth.

Connor's face hardened, his eyes darkening to blackest granite. "Come through. We need to talk about your care."

"Care? What's that got to do with you?"

"Everything," he challenged, his voice no more than a growl.

Connor held the door open wider, and Holly swept through, driven by helpless anger. How dare he think he could discuss her care with a stranger? She'd had enough of that in her lifetime—of other people making all her decisions. She wasn't a child any longer, she was an adult. A strong and capable woman, with responsibilities. A woman who didn't need anyone else.

The doctor sat at her desk, eyeing Holly carefully, as if weighing her words before speaking.

Biting the inside of her lip, Holly sat on the chair Connor indicated, sweeping her legs away to one side when he sat in the seat beside her.

"According to Carmen you need supplements to rebuild your strength, and you need more rest, too. Whatever you've been doing to drive yourself to this state, it has to stop."

"Stop? You can't dictate to me."

"Watch me."

"You have no right. This is my body. My choice. I don't want to bring another unwanted child into this world." Holly felt Connor's body go rigid beside her.

Carmen looked up, a startled look on her face and a hint of censure in her eyes.

His tone was unmistakably feral. "If you think this baby is unwanted, you're wrong. Completely and utterly wrong." Connor rose to his feet. "I'm sorry, Carmen, but Holly and I have some matters to discuss—privately."

"Sure, I understand." Carmen gave him a worried smile before looking at Holly. "Don't rush into any decisions. Obviously the news has come as a bit of a shock—for you both. Connor, I think you have all you need from me today."

"Thanks, Carmen. Yes. I'll call the specialist in the morning."

"Specialist? I can't afford a specialist." Holly wanted to scream—anything to make them pay attention to her. Didn't her opinion matter at all? Her entire childhood people had talked around her as if she didn't exist and, when they couldn't ignore her, as if she didn't matter. She'd fought hard for control of her life—she wasn't about to give that up now.

Connor's strong hand caught at her elbow, urging her from her seat and propelling her towards the door. In his car, Holly sat glowering mutinously out the front window. Instead of starting up the engine, Connor gripped the leather-wrapped steering wheel and turned to her. But for the whitening of his knuckles she would probably never have realised how angry he was. Now tension undulated from his body in waves.

"I'm going to make this perfectly clear right here and right now. You're not handling this by yourself, understood?"

Holly faced him, the burning determination in his eyes making her mouth dry and the words she'd been about to utter in denial fade into obscurity.

"Holly?" He ground out her name as if holding himself in check.

She wasn't going to win this war. Not today. She gave a curt nod. "All right. I understand you."

"Good." Without another word, Connor twisted the key in the ignition and fired the BMW to throbbing life.

She didn't pay a lot of attention to the route he'd chosen to take her back to her house, until she had to flip the sun visor down to block the late-afternoon sun now shining in her face. If they were heading to her place, the sun would be at their backs, not blinding them as it was now.

"This isn't the way to my place. Why aren't you taking me home?" She demanded.

"I am." Connor's hands tightened on the steering wheel.

"This isn't the way to my house," she persisted.

"No."

"Then where are you taking me?"

"To mine."

"To the apartment?"

"No, to the island."

"What?"

"You heard me." Connor turned the wheel of the car, and they swooped down the ramp leading to the basement car park of the Knight Enterprises Tower.

"Why?"

"Holly, be reasonable. You don't even have enough food in your house to eat a decent meal, let alone enough money in your account to go out and buy one."

"You don't know that!" Holly stared at him in horror. How could he know?

He slid the car to a halt in his designated park and turned and raised one eyebrow. While he didn't so much as murmur, he told her in no uncertain terms he knew far more about her than she was willing to say.

"And we need to talk about the baby, and how long you can keep working, if at all." Connor reached across and unclicked her seat belt when she made no move to do it herself.

Shock sent a tremor of fear through her. Her job! She couldn't afford to lose her job. Holly slumped deeper against the expensive upholstery, helpless in defeat.

Connor knew the instant she gave up. It was there in the slump of her shoulders, the droop of her lips, the incline of her delectable, slender neck. All fire, all life, all hope extinguished. A flicker of compassion ignited briefly before he ruthlessly quelled it.

He couldn't afford compassion now, not when his mind still reeled in disbelief. She might never have told him about the baby if he hadn't pushed her. Who knew what crazy decisions she'd have reached on her own, especially given her precarious financial state. Anger roiled violently inside him.

By all that defined him, there was no way anything was happening to his child. The truth had been hidden from him before with disastrous consequences. No way on this earth would he let that happen again.

He exited the BMW, barely managing to resist the urge to slam his door, and walked around to her side to help her from the car. She was about as responsive as a rag doll, a far cry from the woman who'd argued with him at the doctor's surgery—even further from the woman whose passion had ignited in his arms and who'd since invaded his dreams and virtually every waking thought.

As he guided her towards the elevator, Connor flipped his cell phone from his pocket and punched in a few digits. "Thompson, could you arrange dinner for two on the pool patio please." He paused while Thompson, his general factotum at his residence responded. "No, the guest suite won't be necessary. We'll be there soon." He snapped his phone shut.

"I'm coming back tonight?" Holly lifted her head, hope flaring like a struggling beacon in the depths of her dark-blue eyes.

"Why would you think that?"

"Well, you said no extra room." Her voice trailed off, sounding suddenly unsure.

"You're sleeping with me, where I can keep an eye on you." He baled her up with a glare. "At all times."

Like it or not, she'd be sleeping with him. He wasn't taking any risks. Not with something as precious as his baby. He couldn't help the involuntary blistering flood of desire, that pervaded his body. Sharing a bed with Holly would bring its own gruelling brand of torture, but each night his son or daughter would lie secure in his arms. That was a promise.

"I don't recall agreeing to come and stay with you. We're supposed to be talking." She paused, giving emphasis to her next words. "Just talking."

"We'll be talking all right. Don't worry on that score."

"But I still have to stay with you?"

"Yes." He wasn't prepared to negotiate on that one.

He watched as Holly nibbled at her lower lip.

"One night, then. So we can sort things out."

Connor let go of the breath he didn't realise he'd been holding, relieved that he didn't have to answer his own question about what he might have done if she'd refused. But one night wouldn't be enough to satisfy his concerns. He'd do his best to ensure that he was there to protect his child at all times.

Their silent journey to the helipad on the rooftop was uninterrupted. At this late hour of the afternoon most of the staff had already gone home. Holly tried to settle the cascading fear that threatened to tip her over the edge as the elevator sped to the top of the building.

Why couldn't he just leave her alone? The plea rose within her, sharp and powerful, but never made it past the obstruction lodged in her throat. She knew darn well the reason why. Her hand fluttered to her lower abdomen, settling there briefly before dropping back to her side. The baby.

Her baby.

Life couldn't get any worse.

The corporate chopper, a sleek shining black Agusta, custom detailed for Knight Enterprises, crouched with ominous intent on the helipad. The pilot was already at the controls, the rotors swinging in an inexorable circle and boiling up a wind that buffeted stinging dust into Holly's eyes.

Connor drew her close to his side, sheltering her from the worst of the wind with his body, and guided her to the open chopper door. Inside, she clipped her belt, then sat still in her seat, hardly daring to move as her heart began to race and her stomach lurched a fierce warning that it'd had about enough excitement for one day. Although she'd travelled in the Agusta before, she'd never made the short hop to Connor's private sanctum.

"To the island now, sir?"

"Thanks, Dave. Thompson will be waiting for us."

In the darkened cabin Connor levelled a shadowed stare in her direction and a tentative frisson of anticipation licked at Holly's body. He adjusted his headset and gestured to Holly to do the same. She shook her head in denial. She had no desire to hold a conversation with him in this shining display of wealth and prestige, not now while her nerves were so raw. It would take every last ounce of composure to gather her thoughts together for the coming discussion.

To her knowledge Connor had never brought a female guest, who wasn't family, to the island he'd bought after his divorce. A short flight from the central business district, she knew the island was his oasis of peace and tranquillity—a haven he guarded fiercely.

By the time they circled the island and landed Holly felt about as brittle and tightly strung as overstretched fencing wire. One touch, one word, and she'd splinter into a million shattered pieces. She eschewed Connor's assistance to exit the chopper, preferring to make it on her own, albeit unsteady, legs. She ducked and walked as quickly as she could towards the looming two-storied silver-grey stone house several yards in front of them.

Holly counted no less than three chimneys reaching into the twilight sky above the steeply peaked slate-shingled roof.

"This is your home?" she asked, annoyed that she couldn't keep the awe from her breathless voice.

"It's my house. It takes a family to make a home." Connor's jaw tightened as he ejected the words from tensely drawn lips.

Family. How cruelly ironic they both seemed to want what they didn't have. Although, given her current disposition, he'd have his family within the next year, but where would she feature in all that? And did she want to feature anywhere?

Holly clenched her fingers into tight fists, welcoming the physical pain of her nails as they embedded in her palms. The sharp contrast of the tangible discomfort balanced the mental torment that battered at her senses. She didn't want to go down that road. Too much remained unanswered in her life—far, far too much. Right now she had to get a grip on controlling her own destiny—whatever that might be.

Eight

A tall gentleman with silver hair waited at the edge of the patio to greet them.

"Thompson, this is Miss Christmas, who will be staying with me."

"Certainly, sir. I'll take Miss Christmas's things up to the master suite—"

"I don't have a bag." Holly interrupted, adding silently, *I don't have anything. No possessions. No choice. Nothing.*

"I'm sure we can accommodate your needs for one night," Connor gave Thompson a look that demanded an affirmative answer.

"Certainly we can," the other man carried on smoothly, not even a wrinkle of curiosity or concern marring his expressionless features. "I've prepared drinks on the patio for you. Dinner will be brought through in about fifteen minutes if that's all right with you, sir."

"Sounds fine, Thompson. Thank you." Connor pulled out a comfortably cushioned patio chair, "Sit down."

It was more of a command than an invitation. She accepted the chair he offered and gazed around her apprehensively. This really was some place. A subtly lit pool glimmered deep turquoise green over to her left, while cleverly positioned up-lights cast a glow over rough-hewn stone blocks, making the house seem more like a living thing than a building. Subtropical native palms and ferns clustered in the garden while hints of colour could be picked out in the soft night light from lush red begonias and bromeliads strategically planted for effect.

"The garden is beautiful," she blurted, as she accepted a flute filled with sparkling golden liquid. She lifted the glass to her lips, then hesitated. Should she even be drinking alcohol? Lord, she had no idea what she should be doing. While she denied wanting the child, and would do anything to undo the fact that she'd fallen pregnant in the first place, some instinct halted her hand.

"It's sparkling grape juice, no alcohol." Connor sipped his own glass as he leaned back in his chair. "Do you like gardening?" Connor tilted his head to one side. Shadowed as he was, she couldn't make out his expression.

"Well, if I had time I'm sure I would."

Connor forced himself to hold his tongue at her stilted response. Time? She'd have plenty of time in the coming months, he'd make certain of that.

He suddenly realised that even though, as his PA, she'd basically run his days, and many of his weekends, for the past three years, he still knew little about her. Nothing bar what made her eyes deepen and darken in exquisite pleasure and how the cool satin of her skin heated to his touch and flushed a delicate rose in the height of passion.

His groin tightened in flaming response—a response he ruthlessly quashed with sudden loathing at his own unbridled reaction.

"Well, Thompson won't mind a bit of company in the garden if you want to test your green fingers." A sardonic smile played at his lips as she shot daggers of fury from her eyes.

"I hardly think that one night will make any difference to your Mr. Thompson."

The subtle sound of rubber-soled shoes on the slate-tiled patio announced Thompson's return. "Here's our meal. I'm sure you're ready to eat."

"I'm not hungry." Her voice distant, stilted, Holly leaned back in her chair and folded her hands on her lap.

"You *will* have something."

"I can look after myself. Thank you."

"I don't know where you got the misguided idea that you can look after yourself. Look at you. You're nothing but skin and bone. Keep this up and you'll hurt the baby." Ah, now that generated a response. He watched as blue fire flickered in her eyes and she leaned forward, placing her hands flat on the table in front of her, challenge glowing fiercely on her face.

"Well, maybe that's up to me."

Connor bit back the retort that sprang to his lips and forced himself back in his chair. Damn difficult when all he wanted to do was tie her down and force feed her. So, she wanted to jeopardise his baby? If she did, it would be over his dead body.

He needed to try a different tack. He hadn't made his reputation by being bullheaded and intractable. Silently he dished up a small portion of the steaming fluffy white rice onto a plate, then ladled the sweetly scented Thai chicken sauce onto it and set it in front of her, before serving a larger portion for himself.

"Do you remember when you last had something to eat?"

He lifted her fork and scooped up a small bite, holding it in front of her lips. "Go on, try it. It's very good."

He watched as Holly's nostrils flared ever so slightly, inhaling the aroma of the perfectly prepared meal. She moistened her lips with the tip of her tongue and swallowed. Tracking the small movement of the muscles in her neck shot a bolt of electricity through him—an unnerving reminder of another time when he'd felt the play of those muscles beneath his lips, his tongue.

Disgust swamped him, swift and fierce. He didn't need this, or the constant reminders of what they'd shared. She didn't want to eat. So be it. He'd have her hospitalised if necessary. He didn't need to wait on her hand and foot. And then, miracle of miracles, she parted her lips and accepted the food he held poised in front of her. He lowered the fork back to the plate and watched as she methodically chewed, then swallowed.

She dipped her head, not meeting his eyes. "I'm sorry, you're right. The food is lovely. I can manage for myself."

They ate without speaking, accompanied only by the lap of gentle waves in the distance, stroking back and forth on the silver strand of sandy beach visible only a few hundred yards away, and the chirrup of crickets' unobtrusive accompaniment in the background. Enchanting scents swirled around them, borne on the gentle summer night air: Queen of the Night, rich and heady, and the salt tang of the sea a short distance away.

The irony of the beauty of the setting and the romanticism of the night wasn't lost on Holly, who'd surprised herself by finishing the serving Connor had dished for her.

Thompson came to clear away their dishes and replaced them with a slice each of a light and tangy passion-fruit cheesecake, topped with fresh whipped cream and drizzled with mango sauce. Holly had devoured her portion, her taste buds savouring the delicate flavours. Now replete, she sat back and barely managed to stifle a yawn. She looked around with a heavy heart and tired eyes. This would be paradise under any other circumstances.

"You're tired. I'll show you our room."

She jumped at the sound of his voice and looked up to find his eyes still burning into her. Had he taken his gaze off her once this evening? Holly couldn't be certain, but she doubted it.

"We haven't discussed what we're going to do about the…the…" She couldn't bring herself to even say the word *baby* out loud.

"Do, Holly?" Connor spun his coffee cup in his strong capable hands, hands that had driven her to heights of pleasure she had never dreamed imaginable. Hands in which her future now lay.

Holly stifled a shudder. "Yes, we need to talk about it."

"There's nothing to discuss. You're pregnant with my baby. I'll ensure you're accorded the best care possible, and I'll be there when he or she is born."

"What if something goes wrong?" She had to ask. She had heard, somewhere, one in four pregnancies miscarried. Maybe she'd be that one in four. After all, it was early days yet. She had no idea whether there was some abnormality, some genetic predisposition, that would prevent a normal healthy pregnancy. A chill prickled over her skin. She had no idea at all.

"I will do everything I can to make certain nothing goes wrong." Connor pushed his chair away from the patio table and rose to his feet, looming over her in a manner that brooked no argument. "So will you."

"And after the baby is born, what then? What if it's sick, or has some defect or abnormality that you didn't know about. Will you want it then?" Her voice rose uncontrollably as fear of the unknown tore through her like the jaws of a voracious shark.

"Family is everything to me." Connor looked at her as if she'd crawled out from under a particularly slimy rock. "In my opinion only the lowest kind of parent wouldn't want and love their child no matter how perfect or imperfect they are."

"There are some that don't." Holly replied, a tremor belying the emotion that ripped her apart. Parents like her mother, who'd abandoned a perfectly healthy child without reason.

"Some like yourself? Is that what you're saying?" Connor reached up and loosened the knot of his tie. "Well, don't worry, Holly. I will happily bring up my child on my own. I have more than enough love for both of us."

"And what then? What about me?"

"Good question." His face hardened like granite, his eyes bottomless in their hooded darkness. He continued in a voice colder than the Arctic Circle, "You'll be free to go, won't you? That *is* what you want, isn't it?"

Free to go. A shard of ice lodged deep in her chest. She hadn't had a chance to stop to think about what would happen once the child was born. What did she know about motherhood? She'd hardly had a sterling example in her own mother. And what about extended family? As far as she knew, she had none.

The prospect of trying to raise a child terrified her. In the deepest recesses of her memory she had shadowed pictures of a smiling face, an impression of the warmth of another's arms, snatches of a tune hummed in the dark to chase the night terrors away. But the memories were so few and so ephemeral, they may have merely been wishful thinking. And moneywise, even after Andrea died it still wouldn't be easy. Babies cost money, there were no two ways about it. To keep the child, she'd have to work anyway to support day care, leave her baby to a stranger to be raised. To abandon her baby daily to what she'd spent the last eight years trying to forget. Connor could offer this child everything she'd never had, everything except its own mother. With sudden clarity Holly understood what she had to do.

"I take it I still have a job at Knights?"

"Well, we'll have to see about that." Connor sat back in his chair and rubbed his chin with one long-fingered hand. "Why don't you get your strength back first, then we'll discuss it further."

"Oh, really? And tell me, how am I supposed to support myself in the meantime? I've used up all my leave and sick days."

"I'll see to it that you continue to receive your pay. Until the baby's born you won't want for anything. Obviously, I'd prefer you stay here instead of that excuse for a house you've been living in. You'll have everything you need."

A short sharp bark of laughter ejected from her throat. Need? What did he know about need? He had it all in spades. A family, a home. A job. And now this baby. All she had left was her pride and a whole lot of expenses, and her pride was about to take a long walk off a short pier. She had to tell him about Andrea, risk more of his pity. If he didn't understand why the money was so important, she didn't know what to do next.

"This is about more than my comfort. Have you ever heard of juvenile Huntington's disease?"

"Vaguely." His face blanched in the evening light. "Are you saying you're a carrier?"

"No. I don't even have a medical background to check. But my sister—my foster sister—Andrea, has the disease. She's in the last stages and requires full-time care. Very expensive care. That's where my money goes. I can't afford to lose my job.

She'd have to be moved into the public system. I promised her when she was still well enough to understand I would never let that happen. She's all I have. I won't let her down. Not now."

"And you never told me this before. Why exactly?"

"It's my problem. I handle my problems myself. My way." She took a deep breath, filling her lungs with the scents that lingered enticingly on the night air, knowing that with her next words she'd no doubt be damning herself in his opinion of her. Somehow she had to keep her promise to look after Andrea, no matter what. "Her disease is incurable, but there are things she could have to make her more comfortable. Things I can't afford. I'll agree to have this baby for you, on condition that you continue to pay me so I can cover Andrea's fees."

Her words fell like lead pellets on a tin plate, and across the table Connor flinched. He leaned back in his chair, eyeing her as if she'd escaped from a lunatic asylum.

"You're kidding me, right? You want me to pay you, like some surrogate?" His tone implied he expected her to withdraw her words, but Holly wouldn't take them back even if she'd wanted.

She settled more comfortably in her chair, forcing her fingers to relax, to project an aura of calm. "I think I made myself clear."

A muscle worked on the side of his jaw. Clench, release. Clench, release. Holly knew she'd crossed some invisible line to a point of no return. If he'd had an ounce of respect left for her, she'd splintered it beyond redemption.

"I can see why you'd want to help Andrea. But, Holly, you only had to ask me. I'm not a monster."

No, he wasn't a monster, and that was the problem. She was the monster with her hazy past and unnatural feelings about motherhood. Holly felt trapped, vulnerable, exposed.

"Well, like I said. I deal with my problems my way." She fought to remain still in her seat. If she backed down on this, she was terrified she'd lose everything. "And while I'm on the subject of Andrea, if I agree to stay here, I'll still need to see her regularly."

"Fine. I'll see to it that Thompson takes you over to the city in the launch each day, weather permitting. I'll even continue to pay your salary for as long as you're here, with a lump-sum payout after the baby's birth. Give me the details of Andrea's hospital, too. I'll make the necessary arrangements to take over her bills."

Relief flowed through her. With her income unencumbered by Andrea's fees she'd be able to start the investigation into her background she'd always promised herself. After the baby was born maybe she'd even have enough saved to hire someone to find out who she really was, instead of stabbing around in the dark searching public records for any information.

"So, is that everything tied up to your satisfaction? You'll stay?" Connor interrupted her thoughts.

She meticulously refolded her napkin and placed it back on the table, amazed that her fingers weren't shaking. "Actually there's one other thing."

"Really, just the one?" Sarcasm twisted his lips into an ugly line.

"I want a written contract." Holly lowered her hands to her lap and clenched her fingers together until they started to go numb.

"A contract to have my baby. What? You think I'll renege on the deal?"

"That's right." Her mother had, after all, reneged on her. By whatever means possible, Holly would ensure that this baby had at least one parent that could continue to look after it.

He sighed and closed his eyes briefly before opening them wide again and impaling her on the hot anger of his glare.

"A contract to have my baby and then leave."

Leave? She hadn't had a minute to even think that far ahead, but if that's what it took… "Yes." Her voice quavered.

"To never have anything to do with the child again?"

"Yes." Her reply was nothing but a whisper on the sultry evening air.

His expression changed to one of complete and utter disgust. Had she gone too far? Holly felt regret bloom in her chest; wasn't she just as bad as her own mother? She ruthlessly quashed the thought as it gained momentum in her mind, reducing it back into that dark part deep inside where her hurts remained locked away. She wasn't like her mother. She wasn't abandoning her baby to the unknown. Connor and his family would love and cherish this child in ways she'd never known nor knew how to.

"It's a deal." He sounded as though he'd aged twenty years in twenty minutes. "I'll have the papers drawn up immediately."

She looked at him, seeing the man she'd secretly given her heart to—the man she'd given her innocence to—and saw a stranger. Holly inclined her head in acceptance and pushed her chair away from the table, rising onto surprisingly steady legs. She lifted her chin and raised all the composure she could find within her. "I'd like to go to bed now."

Connor's chair scraped roughly across the tiled patio as he, too, rose from the table. "Follow me."

In silence Holly followed Connor inside the house. They passed through French doors into a vaulted-ceilinged room, the high walls lined with bookcases and a highly polished antique partner's desk claimed pride of place on a vibrant, jewel-hued carpet. While modern office equipment, including the latest discreet flat-screen computer, proved this was a working office, there was an elegance and permanence about the fittings.

Only the best adorned his house—his whole life in fact, she reminded herself as the sliver of ice slid deeper into her chest. The baby would want for nothing. She'd made the right choice.

Holly, however, belonged here about as much as a speck of dust on the immaculately polished sideboard in the formal dining room. She was a castoff. Unwanted, unloved and definitely surplus to requirements once she'd completed her duties. But Andrea would be secure in the hospital. With the best of everything Connor Knight's money could buy for as long as it still mattered.

She barely noticed the rest of the house as they passed through a wide, carpeted hallway and through to a sweeping curve of stairs leading to the second floor. She gripped the satin-finished handrail as though it was a lifeline and dragged herself up the stairs in his wake.

The master suite upstairs, which included a private sitting room to one side, overlooked the pool area. Someone, Thompson presumably, had dimmed the exterior lights so only the blue-black hue of the sky, littered with diamond bright stars, was now visible through the open deep bay windows. Filmy net filters, drawn back from the glass, drifted softly on an imperceptible breeze.

The stark contrast of her position, having only the clothes on her back, to his immense wealth and privilege widened the gulf in her mind. Her love for Connor was even more futile now than ever before. Aside from producing his child what use could she possibly be to him once the pregnancy was over? It wasn't as if they would be able to continue to work together. Not even she was that naive.

They had nothing in common. Not background, not education, not position. Somehow she had to rediscover her dignity, her self-respect. Finding exactly how seemed about as insurmountable as her ability to scale Mt. Ruapehu in high heels and a corporate suit.

Connor's voice interrupted her thoughts.

"The bathroom's through there, and beside it the wardrobe." He gestured one arm across the spacious room to panelled doors on the other side. "We can gather your things tomorrow. Thompson will find space in the closet for you. Get some rest. You look shattered." He took a step closer to her, his hand lifting to her face, one finger gently tracing her cheekbone, an unreadable expression locked in his eyes. Holly's pulse jumped in her veins at the tenderness of his touch. She held her breath, too afraid to exhale in case it destroyed the insubstantial sense of intimacy between them. But the intimacy was as far from the real thing as a cubic zirconia from a Kimberly diamond. His hand dropped back down to his side, breaking the tenuous thread of closeness. "We'll talk in the morning."

"You're not coming to bed now, too?" The words blurted from her before she could think.

"I have work to do."

Holly watched Connor go, feeling strangely lost until she reminded herself of her reasons for being here. Any hope she'd harboured that he might still want her in some way, no matter how minute, disintegrated in the face of the harsh reality. She was little more than a baby incubator for him.

The room, huge compared to anywhere she'd slept before, was cavernous without him there to fill the massive space with his presence. She drifted across the floor to the window and looked out at the city twinkling far, far away in the distance.

Weariness dragged desolately at every atom in her body, yet she couldn't bring herself to pull away from the window. It was as if she'd lived a lifetime in one day. Had it only been this morning she'd arrived at work, determined to start the day fresh? She wrapped her arms around her torso in a futile effort to seek comfort from the helplessness that permeated her mind.

Eventually, she wasn't sure how much later, she made her way to the en suite bathroom. A folded white towelling robe had been placed on the large marble vanity next to feminine toiletries, obviously placed there for her use.

Holly peeled away her clothing, letting it drop to the floor in a heap. She didn't care if she had to wear it creased tomorrow. Right now, that was the least of her worries. She gave a longing glance at the deep oval spa bath, big enough for two. She hastily pushed aside the mental image of Connor and her bathing together and tried to quell the heated flush of desire that fought through her exhaustion and struck like an arrow of need from deep within her. It would be foolish to dream, or even imagine, such a thing would ever happen.

Holly thrust open the glass panel door that opened to the shower and twisted the mixer on. Without even waiting for the water to heat she stepped inside the tiled stall and under the cascade of water. Finally she let go the wrenching emotion she'd held banked since Carmen had delivered the news of her pregnancy. The pulsing jets sluiced away her tears until she was empty and could cry no more.

By the time Holly had dried herself and wrapped the soft terry cloth robe around her frame, all she craved was unconsciousness. She didn't want to think anymore. She didn't want to feel. Tomorrow would be soon enough to face her demons.

Some time in the night a sound penetrated her sleep, rousing her enough to open her eyes.

Connor.

She'd left the drapes open, to give her some sense of contact with the familiarity of the city she'd left behind. Now she could see him clearly as he stood, framed in the window, naked. Her body clenched at the beauty of him as moonlight caressed his form. His muscles, like sculpted marble, were thrown in deeper definition by the silver light cast through the window.

Holly squeezed her eyes shut. She couldn't bear to look at him and not want to mould her fingers over each perfect line. To touch him as she'd always dreamed of doing. Yet she knew her hopes and desires were futile. He would no more welcome her attentions than he'd allow her the freedom to return to her house. She was ensnared by her own foolish love. A love that lay in tatters—barren of hope.

She held her breath as she heard him move across the floor and slide in between the divinely soft and faintly scented cotton sheets. All her senses screamed to full alert as he moved across the wide expanse of no-man's land in the centre of the bed, to where she'd curled up far on one side.

His arm, hot and heavy, hooked around her, pulling her to him until, through the towelling robe, her back was infused with the hard heat of his body. She felt the tie at her waist slide loose and the fabric part as he gently pushed his hand past the cloth barrier to her skin.

Her nipples tightened and tingled as his fingers stroked her, cupping the almost nonexistent curve of her belly as if cradling the new life that grew deep inside of her. He was aroused; she could feel the pressure of his erection cradled by her buttocks. Flames licked from her core, setting a hot throb of desire through her. Would he make love with her? Did he know she was awake? Wanting him? Feeling him want her? All she had to do was shift her hips and the short robe would ride a little further and she'd feel him against her.

His hand at her stomach stilled. No longer stroking. Just there. She felt his body relax against hers and heard his breathing settle into a deep even rhythm. *He was asleep?*

Her nerve endings shrieked their disbelief. Her body was on tormented full alert and he'd gone to sleep. It was another slap in the face. Emphatic proof that his interest lay in the baby, and only in the baby.

Gently, then with a little more pressure, Holly tried to push his arm away from across her waist. His breathing didn't alter but she felt the corded muscles in his arm bunch beneath her fingers as he pulled her harder against him.

He wasn't letting go. His strength should give her comfort. She tried to rationalise her fractured thoughts in an attempt to calm the need that spiralled in coils of tension throughout her body.

Instead, pain carved to the depths of her soul—it wasn't her he wanted.

Nine

Connor straightened his tie and slipped into his jacket. The rustle of the lining didn't even disturb Holly as she lay sprawled across the bed.

It was a week since she'd made her outrageous demands reducing herself to nothing but a surrogate bearing his child. A week since he'd learned he'd be a father and watched his child's mother sign away all rights to her natural state. It had sickened him to his heart to see her do so. He'd given her every opportunity that night to argue for her position in their baby's life. But she'd been almost thankful to accept the terms he'd stated, never believing for a minute that she would rescind all rights to him like that or that she'd be just as driven by money as his ex-wife had been.

Once he'd discovered Holly's financial problems were based in her obligations to Andrea, he'd relaxed a little on pressuring the investigator. The dearth of information had been frustrating, anyway. It was as if she'd been born at the age of fifteen, when she'd finally been placed with the family where she'd met Andrea.

Connor reached out his hand and touched Holly lightly on the shoulder. "We have an appointment with an obstetrician this morning. It's time you got up."

She sat upright, her disoriented state lending a charming dishevelment to her normally aloof air. Then the expression on her face, at first slightly puzzled, changed as her skin paled. Her eyes were deep-blue lakes in their sockets. She muffled a tiny moan of dismay behind fingers pressed to her mouth, and he watched, helpless, as she bolted for the bathroom. What had started as afternoon sickness, now dominated her whole day, and he worried incessantly that she wasn't getting enough nutrition.

Connor waited until he heard her rinse out her mouth at the basin a few minutes later. Frustration rippled through him. Every morning for the past four days had been the same, and he hadn't the faintest idea of how to handle it. It galled him to feel so helpless.

He hovered at the bathroom door. "We need to be ready to go in about forty-five minutes. Would you prefer to have breakfast upstairs?"

In the mirror he watched Holly grit her teeth in staunch determination. "I'll be okay. Just give me a minute or two to get dressed."

She lifted her eyes from the highly polished chrome taps and met his stare in the huge bevelled mirror above the vanity. The angry flare of heat reflected there seared him like a brand. His gaze dropped. Bent, as she was over the basin, the generous neckline of her nightgown had fallen open, exposing one creamy swell of breast tipped with dusky rose.

His libido, still stinging from the denial he'd rigorously implemented, clawed at his insides like a starving, roaring beast. His mouth dried and he felt his lips part, almost in remembrance of the night, just over two months ago now, when he'd tasted the intoxicating sweetness of her skin. He should move, say something, do something—anything but stand here, a helpless victim to the siren call of her body.

She swayed slightly, and her knuckles whitened as she gripped tighter at the marble surface, as though that was the only thing holding her up. "Seen your fill for the morning?" she asked acerbically, lifting her chin and watching as his eyes flicked up to meet her angry stare in the mirror.

"Be ready to leave on time." He snapped, mad as hell that, like some hormone-driven teenager, he hadn't been able to control his voyeuristic tendencies and in doing so he'd allowed her the upper hand.

Connor stalked out of the bedroom suite. Holding her to him each night was sweet torture. His hands clenched into fists and unclenched again. As uncomfortable as it was proving to be, she had to remain hands off. He didn't want to crave her like this. He would overcome the incessant desire she'd loosed in him, even if it took every last ounce of control he had left. Denial was nothing new in his life. It made him who he was.

Connor pounded down the staircase and made his way to the breakfast room. His cell phone buzzed in his pocket and he frowned as he identified the number. Euminides Investigations.

"Yeah," he barked.

"I thought you might like to know that your Miss Christmas has put a request into our office."

"A request? What the hell? What sort of request?"

"One identical to yours, mate. Since the file's still active, I wasn't sure if we should take her on."

"Thanks for the heads-up." Connor thought for a minute. Why on earth would Holly be investigating herself? "Keep the enquiry open, and keep me posted on the results."

"And Miss Christmas?"

If Connor told them not to take her on as a client he knew they wouldn't, but then she'd probably go elsewhere and for some reason that filled him with unease. No, he wanted to find out why she was doing this. "Keep her on, too, but I want to see whatever you find first, okay?"

"Sure. I understand."

Connor snapped his phone shut and pushed it back in his pocket. What the heck was Holly up to now?

"Coffee, sir?"

"Thanks, I need it. Miss Christmas will be down shortly. She's a little indisposed."

"Ah, yes, good morning, miss." Thompson stared over Connor's shoulder, a polite smile of greeting pasted on his face. "Your usual tea and dry toast?"

Holly stood at the door, wearing a suit Connor recognised from the office. The stark navy blue, broken only by the slash of her soft cream blouse at the lapels, drained her of colour. She'd scraped her hair off her face in a tight twist that would probably leave her with a headache by lunchtime. Still who was he to care? So long as the baby was okay, that was all that mattered. At least, that's what he told himself. He refused to consider that anything or anyone else mattered as much.

"Thank you, Thompson," Holly answered as she skirted around to the far side of the small, circular table in a clear attempt to put as much physical distance between them as she could, given the cosy bay-window setting of the breakfast room.

"Might I suggest water crackers, miss?"

"Pardon?"

"Water crackers?"

Holly's response only just beat his own. What was Thompson on about?

"I've been doing a little reading. It might give you some relief if you eat a dry cracker or two when you first wake. I'll arrange for a container by the bed for you."

"Thank you." Holly looked uncomfortable. A tiny blush of colour stained her cheeks.

"Don't worry, Miss Christmas, we'll look after you." With a pointed look at Connor, Thompson slid a plate of dry toast onto the table in front of Holly.

Connor snapped open the pages of the daily newspaper loudly enough to make her flinch. Fine, if they wanted to be buddies, so be it. He had one agenda and one agenda only. A strong and healthy child. This time there would be no mistakes.

Holly resolutely munched her way through the dry toast and tea, pleasantly surprised that it seemed to want to stay down. She took her empty dishes to the kitchen bench with a grateful smile. "That was just the ticket, thank you."

"Let me know when you're up to eating something else and I'll make sure it's ready for you. My late wife was quite the treat when she was expecting. Went from one extreme to the other."

If she wasn't mistaken there was a little more than an answering smile on Thompson's face. Compassion now lit his severe features, instead of the frigidly aloof demeanour she'd been subjected to since she'd arrived. A tiny spark of warmth kindled in the pit of her stomach. For what it was worth, she had discovered an ally in hostile territory.

"When you two have finished playing happy families, we need to get on our way." Connor's voice intruded into the atmosphere of the kitchen with the chill factor of a southerly blast of wind direct from Scott Base.

"I'll freshen up and be back down in a few minutes. We have plenty of time," Holly answered defensively. She would show him he didn't call quite all the shots.

Connor had barely said a word during the entire visit to the obstetrician, who'd confirmed Carmen's diagnosis and concurred with her recommendations. They'd set up an appointment schedule, at first monthly, then later fortnightly, for Holly's checkups, but the details had swirled past her like wisps of fog on a winter morning. She couldn't afford to be too interested in what was happening within her body. She couldn't afford to care. She'd take no active part in the procedure for as long as she could help it.

Holly twisted her handbag strap between restless fingers as they approached the helipad where the Agusta waited to fly her back to the island while Connor returned to his office. He was acting like her gaoler, escorting her to the chopper as if he expected her to run away.

She barely acknowledged him as he handed her the headset, then with a curt nod walked back to the building. She caught a tiny glimmer of his silhouette behind the glass, backlit by the door to the elevator, and then the elevator doors slid shut and he was gone. She knew she shouldn't feel so suddenly bereft, it was exactly how she'd insisted it be. Yet for some strange reason tears pricked at her eyes.

The rotors were putting up more vibration than normal, she thought as she gripped her handbag tightly in her lap. Realisation dawned. It wasn't the chopper blades. It was her bag that was vibrating. Her pager. A cold shiver racked her body. There was only one reason that pager would be buzzing. She shoved shaking fingers deep into her bag, her breath catching in her throat as they finally closed around the small, oblong box. She identified the number on the small screen. *Andrea's hospital.*

The whine of the rotors began to change in pitch. It was now or never.

"Dave! Stop!"

"Are you all right back there, Miss Christmas?"

"No, I need to make an urgent call. Can you wait a few minutes?"

"I'll call Mr. Knight back."

"Don't bother him just yet. I won't be long."

"I'll be waiting."

She ducked and raced from the chopper the instant Dave came around to open the door.

"Are you sure you don't want me to call Mr. Knight?" he yelled at her retreating back.

Clear of the helipad, Holly waved in response and headed straight for the elevator, punching the call button as if her life depended on it. Her heart pounded as the doors opened down in the lobby less than a minute later.

"Miss Christmas, can I help you?" Stan, one of the day security guards rose from behind his console at the side of the foyer.

"Stan, I need to use a phone. It's urgent. Do you mind?"

"Not at all, miss. Do you know the number?"

"Off by heart." She gave him a small tight smile and took the handset off the cradle, pressing in the numbers in swift succession.

Two minutes later, Holly replaced the receiver. A knot tightened in her chest. The doctor had come to the phone immediately. He'd been waiting for her call, in itself a bad sign. He'd imparted the news Holly had dreaded most since Christmas. Andrea was slipping away.

"Is there something wrong?" Stan's voice penetrated the silent case of shock that enveloped her.

"I need a taxi." Her voice wobbled as tears threatened to choke her throat.

"Come with me, miss. I'll get one for you from the rank outside."

A belt of hot, humid air hit her like a wall as they left the air-conditioned sanctuary of the lobby and approached the taxi rank outside. Stan pulled open the taxi's door, pushing a validated, prepaid taxi voucher into her hands, and Holly slid into the back seat. As the Knight Enterprises Tower disappeared behind her, she murmured the private hospital's address to the driver, then began to pray as she'd never done before in her life.

Please, please let me not be too late.

"What do you mean she isn't there?" Connor paced his office, shouting at the speaker phone on his desk as if that would refute Thompson's calm information that Holly wasn't back at the island.

"They haven't arrived yet, sir."

"Arrived? Dave should have returned here by now. I'll call you back." Connor buzzed down to the front desk security in the lobby.

"Did you see Miss Christmas leave the building a short time ago?... You did? Find out what taxi company and call them to see where they took her."

What the hell was she up to? Why hadn't she called him? He slapped his hands on his desk and fought the urge to swipe everything off its cluttered surface and to the floor. Their agreement had been quite specific. She wasn't to go anywhere without his okay. He should have known better than to trust her. Once he found her, he wasn't letting her out of his sight.

If he found her.

He sank into his chair. She couldn't go missing completely, he rationalised. He would find her. He would find his baby. No matter what. She didn't have the means or the support to disappear for long.

"What?" he roared as Janet peeked her head around the doorway. A pang of guilt punctured his foul temper as she flinched. "I'm sorry, what is it?" he asked in a level tone, banking the fury that roiled inside him.

"Security didn't get the name of the cab company that you wanted, but Stan said she made a call on his phone before she left. No one's used it since. Do you want him to redial it?"

"I'll do it myself. Make sure nobody touches that phone."

Who could she have called? Dozens of possibilities, none of them making any sense, raced through his mind before he arrived at the ground floor and covered the short distance to the front desk.

"I'm sorry, sir. I didn't know she wasn't—" Beads of perspiration stood out on the elderly security guard's forehead.

"Don't worry, Stan. It wasn't your fault." He reached across the desk and pulled the telephone toward him. "This was the one she used?"

"Yes, sir. No one has used it since."

"Haven View Hospital." The disembodied reply at the other end brought him up sharply. She'd gone to her foster sister? But why? "Hello?" The voice enquired down the telephone line.

He gathered his thoughts together, relieved it had been so easy to track her down. "Has Holly Christmas arrived yet?"

"Yes, she has. Would you like me to bring her to the phone?"

"No, don't worry. I'll be there as soon as I can."

He swiftly replaced the receiver and bolted for the emergency stairwell that led to the basement car park. The BMW's tyres squealed in protest as he roared up the garage ramp.

Haven View was Auckland's most exclusive hospital, he knew that from his own personal experience. After all, the last time he'd set foot in there had been to say a final farewell to his mother when he was eight years old. Despite its lavish surroundings and the expansive gardens outside, it was first and foremost a place where people went to die. He thought he'd forgotten the smells, the atmosphere, the fear. Yet it all came rushing back, as current and clear as if it had been yesterday.

Snap out of it! he growled fiercely at his reflection in the rearview mirror. You're thirty-one years old—not a boy of eight filled with terror. Not some little kid who'd cried to be allowed to go outside and play in the sunshine rather than stay with his father and brothers in the room with a mother he barely knew as anything more than a frail bedridden woman. He'd been too young to understand the cancer that had destroyed the vibrant woman she'd been. He could still see the look on his mother's face, of compassion tinged with sorrow, the sweet smile she'd given him as he'd run from the room the instant his father had given him reluctant permission to go.

His oldest brother, Declan, had found him in the garden a short time later, and the look in his brother's eyes had told him it was too late to ever say goodbye. He'd lost his chance forever. His mother was gone.

An air horn sounded a strident warning from in front, snapping him from the past with an urgency he couldn't ignore. Connor swore and swung his car to one side, narrowly missing the container truck headed through the intersection towards the docks. Focus. He had to focus. He had to find Holly.

The entrance to the hospital had changed, and he almost overshot the driveway in his haste. As he got out of his car and walked up the path to push through the front doors, he fought down the memories that rushed back through him of that other day. He'd never dreamed he'd have to set foot in here ever again.

His unexpected presence commanded immediate attention as the two ladies at reception both approached him at the same time.

"I'm looking for Holly Christmas, I understand she's here?"

"Oh, yes, in the Rose room, second down the hall to your right. Are you family?"

Before Connor could reply, a keening sound struck his ears—so inconsolable it cut through to his nerve endings and made the hairs on the back of his neck rise. A shiver ran the length of his spine. Holly!

He flew down the short hallway, coming to an abrupt halt at the door to a room where Holly lay, sobbing, across the inert form of a young woman. The painfully thin figure in the bed, although clearly ravaged by illness, bore a serenity on her face that gave evidence to the battle she'd borne, and finally won, with her release from life.

The room was cluttered with photo frames on every available surface, yet Connor couldn't tear his eyes from Holly's grief-stricken form as she wept—her sorrow a physical force in the room. Desperate helplessness slammed into him with the power of a freight train. He didn't do emotion. Not this kind. Every muscle in his body tensed with the effort not to leave. One way or another Holly needed him right now. He had to stay. He couldn't walk out on this—on her.

A sudden flurry of activity at the door saw the hurried entrance of two other people, a doctor and a nurse. They spared him a cursory glance, their attention on Holly and Andrea's lifeless form. The nurse gently pulled her away, wrapping Holly in strong arms and holding her tight, while the doctor swiftly examined the dead woman.

"Holly, I'm so sorry," the doctor said in a voice that cracked with emotion. "She's at rest now."

"She was all I had left. *All I had.*" A fresh wave of tears swamped Holly's face as she lifted her head from the nurse's shoulder. Suddenly she became aware of Connor standing by the bed. "*You!* What are you doing here?" The words shot from her mouth like gravel from beneath a spinning tyre. "Can't you ever leave me alone? You don't belong here. Get out. *Get out!*"

"Sir, if you could wait outside for a moment, and give Holly a little time to say goodbye to her sister?" The doctor guided him back out the door, closing it gently behind him, a sympathetic look on his face.

Connor stared at the closed door as helplessness seeped into every cell in his body. He should be in there, with her. Providing comfort. Yet he was the last person on earth she wanted to see.

His acknowledgement of that fact scored deeper than he wanted to admit.

Ten

Wherever Holly turned he was there. At night he held her close to him and cradled her in his arms as she cried herself to sleep, despite her every attempt to remain apart.

Through the mind-numbing fog of loss, she sensed his strong quiet presence behind her, acting as a shield, a support, whatever she needed at any given point in time. Ensuring she had everything.

Everything except Andrea.

The funeral arrangements had been taken care of with the precision of a military engagement. Even Thompson had attended the brief but poignant graveside service, his presence swelling the scant number of staff from the hospital who could make it, together with herself and Connor.

The unfairness that Andrea, who'd been so full of life as a teenager, should be so forgotten emphasised with driving, painful clarity just how alone Holly now was.

Somehow, in the past couple of days, she had learned to lock in the pain of saying goodbye to Andrea. It was better not to love. Not to need. Not to want.

She was alone. Utterly and completely alone.

She thought fleetingly of the child she now carried. Not her baby…Connor's. Under the circumstances it was for the best. It was easier not to flay herself open again.

At the island, Holly drifted aimlessly through the house, before wandering upstairs to the bedroom. In the private sitting room off the master suite, she curled up in a deep armchair that faced the window looking back out to the sea. She'd never thought she'd ever feel so abandoned again, yet the pain and the suffering continued. Andrea's illness had cut her to the bone, but it was nothing compared to the raw screaming pain inside her now.

"Holly?"

She turned at the uncharacteristic hesitance in Connor's voice. He carried a large archive box under his arm. Surely he didn't expect her to work now? He'd assured her that she could take up her duties when she felt ready but that Janet was managing brilliantly in the meantime. With her visits to Andrea and the overwhelming tiredness the pregnancy had wrought she hadn't been in any hurry to take on any more.

"I thought you might like these. You know, to have around you. You can put them around the house if you like."

He put the box in her lap and lifted the lid. Inside, wrapped in layers of tissue, were the photo frames that had filled Andrea's room with the history of their all-too-short time together. Slowly Holly extracted each one and stood them on the long coffee table in front of her.

"Thank you," she whispered.

Connor shifted uncomfortably, his hands thrust deep into the pockets of his trousers. "Do you want to talk about her?"

"What's to tell? She's gone."

He squatted down in front of her, taking the frame she clutched in numb fingers and setting it beside the others before wrapping his hands around hers. The heat of his skin enveloped her chilled hands, warming them through and sending the heat in a slow gentle wave up her arms. She didn't want to feel. It was better to stay numb. Holly tried to pull her hands away, but his hold on her firmed.

"Tell me," he coaxed. He hated seeing her like this—empty of fire, of life. It was as if she'd given up on everything. He'd already spoken at length to the obstetrician, concerned about the effect of her mental distress on the baby, and despite the specialist's assurances, he had to do something to chip her out of the frozen block of ice she'd locked herself into.

He pulled a clean monogrammed handkerchief from his pocket and gently mopped at the tears she hadn't even realised she'd shed. "You never listed her on your company profile as a contact in lieu of next of kin. Why?"

Holly sighed and leaned her head back against the cushioned fabric, casting her mind back to the first time she'd met Andrea. It was so unfair that, aside from herself, there was no one left to remember what Andrea had been like before she'd become ill. Maybe if she could share some piece of her past, instead of locking it all inside, it would help keep Andrea alive in someone else's memory for a little longer. Holly drew in a deep settling breath.

"I was fifteen when I was fostered by the Haweras. I thought they'd be like all the others, happy to help until I got into trouble more times than they could cope and then wash their hands of me. But no. They kept coming back to bail me out of trouble, until one night Andrea, who'd been with them already for about a year, told me how much it was hurting them all, her included, to see me trying to destroy myself.

"I'd never seen it through anyone else's eyes before, but she made me believe that they saw something in me that was worth something. Worth keeping. No matter what I threw at them, they stayed right there beside me, until eventually it was easier to want to please them than to make them angry."

"When did she get sick?" The hospital doctor had explained to him the nature of Andrea's illness and its insidious, slow progression. He'd been stunned when he realised Holly had borne the financial and emotional burden alone for so long. It showed a side of her he'd suspected lurked beneath the aloof surface she presented the rest of the world. But why, then, had she given up all rights to her baby? For someone who'd so obviously clung to the one person who had loved her in return, why would she relinquish the chance to share that with a child of her own?

"She started showing early symptoms when she was about sixteen. She went from being a happy girl to having massive mood swings, and her grades at school started to slide. At first I thought it was my fault for being a bad influence, or for not being supportive enough. But then we realised it was more than that. Bit by bit over the years, we lost her. The Haweras did what they could, but it was far more than they could handle financially. Soon after I started work at Knight's, they were killed in a car accident. I took over everything for Andrea at that point. But it was never enough."

Holly pushed up from the chair and stood in front of the picture window, staring at the rolling lawn that stretched to the small private golden beach and the sparkling blue water that lay beyond. "Did you know that if you carry the Huntington's gene there's a fifty percent chance of passing it on to your children?"

"No, I didn't. Is that what's bothering you about the baby? Do you think you might carry the gene?"

"I don't know."

"She was your foster sister, not your blood relative. You probably don't even have the disease in your family."

"But that's the problem." She spun away from the window, pain and fear etched on her face, in her eyes. "I don't *know*. If it's not that disease it could be any one of hundreds of others. Have you any idea of the number of genetic disorders people face every day? I have no idea about my background. Nothing. I don't even know my real last name. I'm terrified I'm about to bring a child into this world only to watch it suffer like Andrea suffered!" Holly's voice grew more frantic with each syllable.

So that's why she'd started her own investigation. Suddenly it all made perfect sense. The wretched fear in her eyes ripped at Connor like a physical threat as the enormity of her dread became more real with every word. This was his baby they were talking about. His flesh and blood. The concept of bringing a child to life—a precious young life— then watching it slowly die while you stood helpless on the sidelines was as foreign as it was abhorrent to him. After watching her foster sister die no wonder she was so frightened, so opposed to bearing a child.

"The baby will be okay." He forced the words out like a mantra. If he said it with enough strength, enough belief, it would be so. Fate wouldn't be so fickle as to take another baby away from him. It wouldn't dare. They'd undergo every test available to be sure.

To lend weight to his words, Connor stepped closer and deliberately cupped his hands on either side of her neck and drew her closer. Face-to-face. Her eyes were still awash with tears and a tiny frown furrowed between her eyebrows. He leaned forward and pressed his lips against the puckered skin.

"Don't worry," he murmured. "Nothing will happen—to either of you. Trust me."

"You can't be sure of that. No one can." Her voice wobbled with uncertainty.

"I protect what's mine." He rested his forehead against hers and slid one hand down to press gently against her lower abdomen. "And this *is* mine."

"Andrea was my life. Don't you understand? I don't know how to go on. I can't do this." The plaintive cry in her voice struck him at his heart.

"You have to go on. One second…one minute…one day at a time. You're alive. You have a new life growing inside you." He spread his fingers possessively across her belly.

"It doesn't seem real. I don't want to believe it's real."

"Believe it, Holly. You. Me. The baby. Very real."

Suddenly words were not enough. He needed to imprint the truth on her. To make her see, to feel, to finally understand, that to distance herself from their baby was useless. He tilted his head and captured her lips, teasing her mouth open, and swept his tongue inside—plundering, imprinting himself upon her. Need burned through him like a flash fire, and he slid his arms around her still-slender waist, pulling her closer until she lined up against the hardness of his body and the softness of her breasts pressed against him.

It wasn't enough. A shudder rocked through her body as he kissed her, and a surge of triumph swelled from deep inside as her arms crept around him, her hands sliding up his back, her nails digging into his shoulders as he suckled on her tongue.

He reached for the buttons that fastened the front of her blouse, fumbling in his desperation to feel her without any barriers, to taste her creamy softness. As the panels swung free he reached behind to unfasten her bra and pushed the lace fabric up—groaning against her mouth with delight as her breasts filled his hands. He rubbed against her tightened nipples with the flats of his palms and felt her lips tremble beneath his.

"Too much," she protested, her legs buckling. "I...feel... too much."

Connor swept her into his arms, and in a few short strides laid her on the bed. Her skirt worked its way up around her hips as he settled his body gently between her legs feeling the cradle of her hips cup his sex. He'd read that her breasts might be more sensitive, that she might even recoil from his touch.

"Tell me to stop," he whispered against her nipple.

He twirled his tongue gently around the darkened aureole then blew gently and watched as it tightened and peaked even harder, goose bumps prickling on her pale skin. He repeated the movement, first warm and wet, then a soft cool breath, wrenching a sound from her that was half plea, half sigh. His lips teased into a smile as he shifted his attentions to her other nipple. She squirmed against him, pushing her hips up to strain against his erection and sending a shaft of desire so deep he had to halt his ministrations to catch himself, to slow down.

But she wouldn't let him slow down. She pulled his head down to her breast and ground her hips against him as, at first gently, then with a steadier pressure, he began to suckle at her sweet flesh. He felt her body wind tighter and tighter, until she bowed against him, her head thrown back in supplication. He tilted his pelvis against her, pressing his aching shaft against the apex of her thighs, against the dampness and heat that shimmered from her core.

He lifted himself away from her before he lost control completely and gently slid his thumb inside the elastic leg of her panties and further until the pad of his thumb rested against the heat of her soft hood of flesh. Slick with her wetness, his thumb swept a lazy circle around her, increasing in pressure as he decreased the tiny spiralling journey.

He laved his tongue again around one nipple before closing around the taut peak and pulling it gently past his teeth and deeper into his mouth. He felt the ripples of climax begin from deep within her, radiating out until she shattered against him before collapsing back into the mattress. Alive. Real.

He released her nipple from his mouth and pressed gentle kisses against her rib cage, trailing down to her waist, her belly. The skirt had to go. It was entirely too much clothing for what he needed now. He dispensed with the zip fastening and slid the black fabric from her and pulled her panties away from her limp body, throwing them both to the floor in a heap.

If he never saw her wear black again it would be too soon.

He pulled up onto his knees and wrenched his shirt off, sending buttons flying in his haste to bare his skin, to feel hers. In seconds he'd discarded the last of his clothing, freed at last. She lay still on the bed. Her eyes glazed, not with tears but with satiation. Her skin flushed a soft delicate pink.

Holly's heart was beating nineteen to the dozen. Her entire body zinged with energy. With life. Connor had rent open the floodgates of feeling, of need and desire, and she wanted more—she wanted him.

She watched as he ripped away his clothing with little attention to care. She pushed herself upright and onto her knees and shrugged off her blouse and bra, letting them slide off the side of the bed to the floor. She didn't want to think. She simply wanted.

Holly reached out and trailed her fingers across the expanse of his chest, intrigued to watch the muscles beneath the surface of his bronzed skin ripple and tighten in answer to her touch. His reaction lent her power. She did this to him. She governed how hard, or soft, she touched him.

She let her nails scrape across his nipples, at first gently, then stronger, harder. At his sharply indrawn breath she looked up, the expression on his face reminding her he was a man, not merely a body. Their eyes linked as she circled his nipples with her nails, bearing closer and closer to the tender, puckered discs. He held his arms rigid at his sides, and she sensed the restraint he employed in keeping them there. In allowing her this discovery of him.

She parted her lips and ran her tongue first along the bottom, then the top. Then slowly, deliberately, she leaned forward and pressed them, swollen, hot and wet, against him. She felt his reaction in the tremors he fought to control. She dropped her hands to his fists, gently imprisoning them against his hips while she kissed his nipples and trailed a moist line of heat down the crease between his rib cage, then lower to his belly.

The dark hair that circled his belly button matted under the onslaught of her lips and her tongue, and again she felt that surge of power, of energy, of life. Reluctantly she pulled away and dropped one leg over the edge of the bed, bearing her weight on it before sliding the other to the soft carpet on the floor.

"Lie down," she commanded. Was that her voice? That husky, sultry, sexy demand. Desire arrowed sharp and true to her centre and radiated out starbursts of fire.

To her surprise he did so without argument, and she climbed back onto the bed, placing one knee on either side of his thighs. A tiny burst of insecurity bloomed inside her. What was she doing behaving like a wanton?

His dark eyes narrowed to slits, and he watched her as she hesitated, his sensual lips immobile as she gazed upon his body. The mute challenge in his eyes dared her to go further, to touch and take him as *she* wanted to. Without severing visual contact she arched her back and lifted her arms to loose the final strands of hair that remained caught in the twist she'd restrained them in.

The long, dark length of silk swung free, and she leaned forward, letting the strands stroke along the inside of his thighs and higher to where his arousal jutted hungrily. Lowering her head, she caught a hank of hair, wound it softly around his shaft and pulled gently upwards watching, intrigued, as the hair tightened around his swollen head before sliding, teasingly over the tip. She repeated the action, suddenly feeling more wanton and far more aroused than ever before.

A pearl of moisture appeared at the tip of his penis. Without thought, driven purely by sensation, she lowered her mouth to him and flicked her tongue across his straining flesh. The taste of him sent a thrumming pulse through her body. She could barely believe her daring. She could barely believe his restraint.

Between her thighs his legs vibrated with tiny tremors. She could feel the suppressed power in him even as he allowed her to play her sensual game with his body. The fact that he even permitted her this supremacy over him burned like a white-hot catalyst, and Holly lowered her mouth again, this time closing her lips over his erection, her tongue playing against the very tip, swirling, tasting, suckling him. His passion-filled groan empowered her even further as she took him deeper into her mouth, amazed at her boldness, terrified by her might.

"Stop!" he demanded, and his hands slid to her hair pulling her gently away from him.

"Did I hurt you?" she asked, instantly remorseful.

"No. But not being inside you is killing me." He swept her off his body and rolled, tucking her beneath him, settling the hard and heavy length of his sex against her. "Open for me," he demanded, his voice as rough as gravel, his eyes consumed by darkness.

He didn't need to ask twice. Holly parted her thighs and lifted her hips to meet him, quivering as he entered her and tightening against the strength of his body. If she thought she had any control now she was seriously kidding herself, she realised, as Connor withdrew slowly from her before sinking to the hilt again, grinding his hips against her, inflaming her body. Saturating her mind with sensation after sensation. He pulled away and plunged again, this time lowering his lips to hers and parting her mouth, taking her tongue inside his mouth and pulling against it in the same rhythm.

Her entire body tensed, aflame with feeling and sharply aware of the taste of him, the feel of him, her complete and utter acceptance of his right to be inside her, to be part of her.

Pleasure built with increasing force as his hips ground against her again. No, it was too soon, too much. And then there was nothing but the sensation of intense satisfaction as it rolled through her body, building and building until she cried out with the intensity and bowed against him, cleaved to him, became part of him as he was a part of her.

Deep in the recess of supreme satisfaction, she felt his body grow taut as with a final thrust he breached his own peak and spilled himself into her body until finally, shaking, he lowered himself against her, taking them both into the softness of the mattress and the limbo of the aftermath of their passion.

The late-afternoon sun slanted through the window, bathing them in a golden glow and drying the perspiration on their bodies. Holly didn't know that she'd ever felt so complete. Connor shifted slightly, taking his weight off her, and tucked her into his side. It struck her in that moment, she was nothing against his will. It didn't matter what he said or what he did. She loved him, and compounding that love she now carried his child.

Instead of the usual terror rising inside her at the thought of bearing a baby, a sense of warmth and wonder permeated her mind as for the first time she allowed herself to wonder, to dream. What would their baby look like? What would it be?

Languidly she curled into Connor's body, relishing the warmth, the security. She was no fool. She knew it wouldn't last. It couldn't. But for now she could allow herself to pretend.

She drifted off to sleep, locked in the curve of his arms. Maybe, just maybe, she could cope with tomorrow and the day after that.

Connor stirred and opened his eyes slowly. The sun had long since begun its traverse to the other side of the world, and now the bedroom was dark, with long moonlit shadows drawn across the carpet. He inhaled deeply, taking in the scent of Holly's hair, her skin, the residue of their carnal fervour, and felt his body rouse all over again.

Not yet, he commanded, willing his body to submit to his command, but it was useless. She'd invaded his senses like an aphrodisiac, feeding the craving he'd duelled with, and lost against, since the first addictive taste of her body.

Beside him, she slept deeply, her whole body relaxed for the first time since he'd brought her here. She needed rest far more than she needed to be woken right now. Connor forced himself to ease his body away from hers and to slide from the bed, pausing to pull the covers over her delectable body, then he padded quietly to the en suite. Closing the door behind him, he flicked on the lights before reaching into the shower stall and wrenching on the faucet, leaving the setting at cold. He couldn't afford to indulge in his baser needs again tonight.

Even though it had been his choice, looking after Holly in the past few days since her sister had died had eaten into him in a way he'd never expected. He had no desire to explore how devastated she was at losing Andrea or how her loss had reminded him of his own desolation at his mother's death. The only way he'd known how to manage her grief, and his own, was to keep going. To force, to cajole—to place one foot in front of the other to get through every day.

Until today. Today she'd passed a boundary he hadn't even realised existed. In some ways it was as if by actually letting Andrea go, in saying goodbye, she'd allowed herself to move forward, albeit with unrelenting encouragement from him.

He stepped into the shower, hissing through clenched teeth as the stinging cold spray assaulted his body, chilling his ardour, and tried to focus his mind instead on the files he'd brought home. He needed to toughen up. To put her back into that corner of his mind where reason mastered sensation and where logic beat attraction. Connor snapped off the stream of cold water with a determined twist of his hand. He had to get back to work.

And yet he still craved her like an addict needed a fix.

Eleven

Holly heard the chopper blades agitating the air. Connor was home. She hadn't even heard him leave for work. After their lovemaking yesterday she'd slept soundly in their bed, right through until morning. The rest had done her good and she didn't feel anywhere near as unwell when she'd risen, although the flask of hot weak tea and the dry crackers she'd found on the bedside table this morning had probably helped, too.

She'd spent the day sorting through the pictures Connor had brought, reliving happier days when she and Andrea could laugh together. Most of the frames she'd wrapped in tissue and put away, until later. Until a time when she'd have her own place again. Only one picture stood on her bedside cabinet under the lamp—a joyful remembrance of Andrea and her at the beach before the symptoms of the disease had begun to show, both of them smiling and full of good health and dreams of the future. It suited Holly that it would be the last thing she saw at bedtime and the first thing she saw when she awoke.

For the rest of the day Holly had wandered around the gardens and taken a swim in the pool. It had been so long since she'd taken some exercise, the swim had left her feeling enervated and she'd drifted off to sleep in a deck chair on the patio. On waking, a couple of hours later, she found that Thompson had positioned a sun umbrella to protect her from the sun's biting force, and a light cotton throw rug now protected her from the gentle sea breeze that blew in from the ocean.

She'd woken feeling deliciously decadent. Never in her life had she ever had the luxury of doing simply nothing. Although it certainly had its appeal, and was allowing her to catch up on much needed rest, she knew she'd be driven crazy with boredom before long. As far as the house was concerned that was entirely Thompson's domain. He saw to the cleaning and the cooking. She hadn't even done so much as her own laundry since she'd been here. She had to talk to Connor about being allowed to do something, anything, to keep her mind active and alert.

He looked tired, she thought as she watched him alight from the Agusta and walk towards the house, his briefcase buffeting against his legs from the wash of air from the rotors. Even looking as tired as he did, he still made her heart race. Their lovemaking last night had sated her senses, yet just one look at him now and she wanted to press herself against him and peel away the corporate layers that turned her lover into the aloof and sophisticated lawyer he was.

She forced herself to ignore the tingling in her breasts and the heat that uncoiled slowly between her thighs and stepped forward to welcome him home.

"Bad day?" she asked, handing him a glass of chilled water with a twist of lime juice.

He looked hot and bothered and downed the drink at once. There was something very sensual about watching a man drink with such thirst, Holly realised, her own throat growing dry in response. The muscles in his strong brown throat drew her gaze, working in a steady rhythm as he pulled at the liquid and drew it down deep into his body. He took the glass away from his mouth, leaving a shining film of water slicked across his lips. She accepted the glass back from him, trying desperately not to stare at his lips or to wonder what they would taste like right now, this minute.

"Thanks, yeah, you could say that. I have a lot of work to get through before tomorrow. Can you ask Thompson to serve my dinner in my office?"

His dismissive rejection of her presence couldn't have been more emphatic. Hadn't last night meant anything to him?

"Surely you can stop to eat. You'll need to take a break to stay fresh."

"Can't afford to." He walked across the patio towards the house.

"Connor!"

He stopped in his tracks and turned slowly, his black eyebrows pulled together in a forbidding frown. "What is it, Holly? I told you I have a lot of work to do. Can't this wait?"

She baulked for a moment; very few people dared press him when he wore that particular look. But she dared. She had to or she'd go mad with boredom. "Maybe I could help you?"

His right hand fidgeted, always a give away when he was irritated. "No. You need to rest. You're still too pale."

"Rest?" Anger swirled like a red haze through her mind. "I've been resting all day. I want to do something. I *need* to do something or I'll go crazy."

"Go read a book, watch a movie."

"I want to help you." He just didn't get it, she thought in frustration. After spending her day wandering around like a lost soul, she'd looked forward to him coming home. The prospect of an endless evening with only her own company stretched before her like an echoing void.

"I said no. Look, if you really want to do something to fill your days, pick a room upstairs and turn it into a nursery. We're going to need it eventually. Maybe the turret room, since that's closest to the master suite, then the nanny can have the room next to it."

"Nanny?" The word *nursery* had been enough to turn her blood to ice in her veins, but *nanny* elicited a gut deep response she didn't want to identify.

"For when you're gone, Holly." Connor explained with pseudo patience. "I'm going to need a nanny."

He turned and went inside. His exit hit her like a physical slap, and Holly sank to the chair behind her. Hearing him speak of a nanny in such cold and clinical terms brought the reality of this pregnancy back to her in spades. A cold clammy shiver ran down her back. She was only here to have his baby and then move on, he'd reminded her quite succinctly. He neither expected nor, obviously, wanted her to stay. And why would she? She hadn't the faintest notion of how to be a mother. Her own had abandoned her so she had no role model there, nor had the succession of foster mothers over the years touched her heart.

The risk of pain was just too great. Losing Andrea had proven that. It was much better to lock those feelings down. Look at what loving Connor had given her. Only more heartache, and now a child she didn't want to love—just as her mother had so obviously not wanted her.

But wouldn't she be doing the very same thing as her

mother? Wouldn't she be just as wilfully neglectful by walking away from her baby? No, it wasn't the same. Not the same thing at all. She propelled herself out of the seat and hurried back inside. Her baby would be loved and would be cared for. It would lack for nothing. *Nothing but a mother's love,* the insidious voice in the back of her mind taunted.

She didn't want to deal with this, not now, not ever, she thought irrationally even while knowing that at some stage she was going to have to. Nature had its own way of making a person sit up and take notice. So Connor wanted a nursery for his baby. Well, she'd give it to him. It would be the best nursery on the planet, just as she'd been the best PA he'd ever had. She'd show him it didn't matter to her. She'd show him she could do this and then walk away. No matter what.

Connor leaned back in his chair and looked through the closed French doors to the patio where Holly still stood, her face partially obscured by the long late-afternoon shadows. He tilted his chair and rested his head against the high leather back.

Why had he baited her like that? What had he expected? That she would suddenly develop overwhelming maternal instincts and demand that *she* be the one caring for the baby and not some nameless faceless stranger? And what did it matter to him, anyway? It wasn't as if he expected her to stay. To be a mother. To be a real family. Life was complicated enough without that.

Truth be told he'd been looking forward to coming home tonight, to seeing Holly. Yet, when he'd seen her all he could think about was her absolute rejection of the child she carried. This morning, before work, he'd almost toyed with the possibility they could have a normal relationship. Be a couple.

But it was hopeless—the mere thought ridiculous—that

was as clear as the nose on his face. Her expression when he'd suggested she create the baby's nursery had been filled with horror. There was no way she'd take on the task. Regret tinged with an emotion even more intangible, knotted in his gut.

He sat upright and flicked open his briefcase. Caring for Holly, beyond seeing to her good health and welfare was not an option. Going down any other road, unthinkable. He'd cared about his mother and she had gone. He'd cared about his wife, and she'd betrayed his deepest trust, totally and irrevocably.

They said you couldn't control who you loved or who loved you. Well, maybe the latter was true, but he had news for the former. He could and would control whom he loved, and right now that began and ended with his baby.

When Connor arrived home the next evening Holly wasn't waiting on the patio with an ice-cool drink. Even Thompson, instead of being in the kitchen putting the finishing touches to the evening meal, was nowhere to be found. Connor flung his briefcase behind his desk in his office and sank down into his chair when a loud hollow thud sounded from the second floor—a thud that sounded sickeningly like someone falling. He hurtled from his seat and headed up the stairs, taking them two at a time.

"Holly!" he shouted as he rounded the landing at the top, his heart hammering in his chest. He tried to tell himself it was just the baby he was worried about, but he had to be honest with himself. It wasn't. Not anymore.

"Holly!" he shouted again, and sagged in relief when he heard her muffled voice.

He raced towards the turret bedroom, the one he'd suggested as a nursery the night before. The door was closed and another thump echoed under the door. As he reached his hand to the doorknob he heard something he hadn't heard before. Surely that wasn't Thompson laughing? The door opened abruptly beneath his hand and swung inwards.

The carpet had been rolled back from the polished floor and the heavy carved wooden furniture in the room was all shoved in the centre and draped in dust covers. Thompson, wearing a baggy set of coveralls, was on his hands and knees, sanding the foot-high moulded skirting boards.

Holly, to his horror, stood on a makeshift scaffold, a scraper in her hand, and balanced precariously on a plank that to his eyes looked far too narrow. A strip of wallpaper hung drunkenly from the wall. She turned, twisting to see him, simultaneously losing her balance and sending the narrow plank skittering to the floor. Connor leapt forward to catch her in his arms and held her against him before lowering her feet to the floor.

His heart beat double time. "What the hell are you doing?" he demanded. A fierce wave of anger swiftly replaced the fear that had torn through him when he'd seen Holly lose balance.

She pushed away from him and free of his hold. Her eyes sparkled and colour flushed her cheeks. A strand of long dark hair had worked free of the crooked ponytail she wore. A smudge of paint dust streaked across her forehead. Connor lifted a hand and wiped it away and watched as her expression froze and changed from one of relief to defensiveness.

"What do you mean, what are we doing? You have eyes in your head don't you?" She turned and defiantly replaced the plank and stepped back up onto it. "We're preparing a nursery."

"Not now you're not." Connor stepped forward and lifted her back down off the makeshift trestle. "It's too dangerous."

"Oh, don't be so ridiculous. If you hadn't burst through the door and startled me like that I would never have fallen. Besides, Edgar is here with me."

"Edgar?" Did she mean Thompson?

"Yes, sir. I offered to do the wallpaper, but in light of my frozen shoulder, Miss Christmas insisted she do it." Thompson levered up from his knees and stood as he spoke, brushing clouds of dust off him as he did so.

Thompson had a frozen shoulder? He'd never so much as complained once. What the hell was going on?

"Well, whatever the two of you have decided to embark on together it stops right now. I'll get contractors in." He spun Holly around to face him. "And the most risky thing you will do from now on is choose paint and fabric swatches."

"Excuse me, I think I'd best go and finish dinner while you discuss this." Thompson edged past the bristling pair and disappeared down the hall.

"There is nothing further to discuss," Connor said through clenched teeth. He wheeled around and stalked from the room, fury building up inside him until he felt as if he'd erupt into a seething, spitting cauldron of molten metal.

The solid thump of the wooden-handled scraper hit him square between the shoulder blades and stopped him in his tracks.

"How *dare* you dictate to me like that?" Holly's voice followed with equal force.

He turned slowly, his hands fisted on his hips. "I dare because you endangered my baby. Remember? The one I'm paying you to have."

"You can't wrap me in cotton wool! Make up your mind for goodness sake. First you tell me to decorate a nursery, now you tell me I can't. Well I have news for you, Connor Knight, and it's all bad. I'll decorate that room if it kills me. You've taken my job from me. You've taken my home from me. You will not take my will away from me, too."

Her eyes flashed, burning blue like heated cobalt. Connor closed the distance between them, aware of the emotion that poured from her, of the way her breasts heaved under an old T-shirt he thought he'd discarded years ago. The worn white cotton draped over her, shaping to her gently rounded shoulders—the sleeves coming halfway down her arms. She looked soft and feminine and extremely desirable. Rigidly he slammed the brakes on his thoughts before they further roused his disruptive libido.

"I don't want to take your will away from you. I just want to keep the baby safe."

"That's all I am to you, isn't it? Just some damn incubator for your blasted baby! What about me? Me?"

She raised her hands and pressed against his chest, vehemently emphasizing each word, and pushing him back a step. Connor caught her wrists before she wound up for another push.

"Stop! Holly, stop!"

"No! I don't want to stop. I can't live like this with you dictating everything I do. I can't wait to get away from here— away from you!"

Her eyes washed with tears. They were his undoing. Maybe he'd been too dictatorial. But she didn't understand what was at stake, or why this child was so important to him. But she was wrong, he realised with damning clarity. She was more than just an incubator for his baby. Somewhere along the line she'd inveigled her way into a crack in his heart. A crack that was opening to let her into a piece of him he fought to hold apart.

If he wanted to be totally honest with himself right now, his first thought had been about the potential danger to her. He hadn't even been thinking about the baby when he'd seen Holly twist and begin to fall. Even now, just thinking about

it—the startled look in her eyes, the position of her body—
made him feel sick to his stomach.

As he held Holly's hands and looked down into her face,
tears pooled in her lower lids and one by one spilled over her
lower lashes to track twin trails down her smooth cheeks.

He didn't want to admit that he cared for her, nor the vulnerability it would leave him open to. Loving his unborn baby
was simple. There could be no lies between them, no trust
broken. Loving Holly was not an option.

Warily he let go her hands and took a step backwards.
Anything that created some barrier between them had to be
good, even if it was only a short, air-filled distance.

"Okay, I admit it. I overreacted. But I mean it about the
contractors. I will get them in to do the basics." He saw her
stiffen, and rushed on before she could interrupt. "To do the
basics only. The rest you can do yourself."

"Define the rest."

"Anything that you can safely reach without requiring assistance like ladders or that wretched scaffolding you put up.
Is that completely clear?"

"Yes."

He turned to walk away, pulling his jacket off and tossing
it onto the bed. The evening sun glinted on the metal edge of
the wallpaper scraper where it had landed on the floor. He bent
to pick it up and turned to face Holly. "I believe this is yours?"

A wash of pink coloured her neck and upwards to her
cheeks. She put out her hand to accept the scraper. "I'm sorry.
I overreacted, too."

Connor held onto one end of the scraper even as she held
the other. "Truce?"

"Yes," she whispered again, this time with her eyes fixed
on the carpet between their feet, as if she was ashamed to meet

his eyes. She'd caught her lower lip between her teeth, biting down hard enough that all colour fled their usual rosy fullness.

Connor tugged gently on the scraper, pulling her slightly off balance and into his arms. Her surprise at being pulled off centre made her let go her lip, and he watched as colour returned to the soft membrane.

He had to taste her.

He lowered his head and drew her more firmly into his hold. She tasted of a heady combination of salt and dust. But more than that, she tasted of her incredibly individual and enticing sweetness and spice that left him constantly craving for more.

Reluctantly he let her go. Any more of this and it would get to be a habit. He had to remember why she was here and how temporary it was. Remember who she was and the fact she was prepared to walk away from their child without so much as a backward glance. A man didn't love a woman like that.

Love?

A wave of denial swamped him. No way. There was no way he'd let himself love Holly. His son or daughter, no matter how perfect or imperfect, would see the light of day. Would feel the warmth of its father's arms, would know—every single day of its life—the love that was for his child and his alone. He had no room in his heart to love another.

He turned away abruptly, wrenched off his tie and yanked at the buttons on his shirt on his way through to the en suite. It had been a day of pure chaos in the office. Janet was good at her job, but she wasn't Holly. The calm and controlled order he'd taken for granted each day had gone to hell in a hand basket, and it didn't look as if it would improve anytime soon. He needed a stiff drink and dinner, and then enough work to ensure he'd fall asleep exhausted, immune to the temptation of wanting to slide inside her body and slake the hunger she set alight in him.

As he'd driven himself to the top of his field, he'd learned to recognise weakness in all its forms and to identify his opponent's Achilles' Heel. He'd honed the ability into a sixth sense and become a master at capitalizing on it, using it to his advantage, then driving home an unbreakable deal.

Now, suddenly, he identified weakness in himself. And he hated admitting he'd allowed himself to become vulnerable to the one woman he couldn't love.

Twelve

Holly stepped back from the curtain she'd just straightened—her heart swelling with pride. She'd painstakingly learned to sew and she'd made them herself, just like she'd made the comforter for the crib and the layette for the bassinette right down to the miniature sheets. She reached forward and gave the drapes a tiny flick, smoothing an imaginary hitch in the fall of the fabric.

Seven months ago she'd never have imagined she could turn into such a homebody let alone furnish an entire nursery. Once Connor's contractors had finished wallpapering and painting the room, she'd had carte blanche to use whichever interior designer she wanted to create the baby's room. Yet, for some reason, it had become more important than she'd ever imagined to leave an indelible print behind her. To leave a piece of her heart.

She reached for the framed picture of the baby's first

sonogram that Connor had placed on the tallboy, trailing her finger across the tiny form captured in black and white. She could still see the wonder that had spread across his face when he'd caught his first glimpse of his child, still see the unsettling and uncharacteristic shine of tears in his eyes. Up until then, she'd hardly had the nerve to look at the radiographer's screen, yet the love that shone from him as he viewed his baby had forced her to turn away from him and look for herself. It was easier to look at the object of his love than to admit that love could never be shared with her.

Holly took a final look around. While she'd been oddly loath to finish the room, taking her time on small details no one but herself would notice, Connor's reluctant yet urgent departure for the States a week ago had been the catalyst that drove her to complete it.

This would be the last time she would come in here. Her end of the deal was all but finished. As if to acknowledge her hard work a tiny foot pressed against her rib cage. Absently she massaged her swollen belly.

With the baby's due date only three weeks away, the days now stretched emptily before her. Holly turned and walked out. A ragged sigh dragged past the sudden tightness in her chest as she closed the door behind her. The day she'd have to leave the island, leave Connor, permanently drew closer with every cross on the calendar.

He'd miss her checkup tomorrow she realised with a pang. He'd made all her doctor's visits thus far, hovering like a worried shadow at every stage of the pregnancy. The baby was everything to him. She'd given up hoping he'd forget for just one moment that she was carrying his baby and see her as a woman with needs and desires again. Sleeping with him every night was fraught with hopes of what might have been, but still he made no attempt to touch her, unless it was to feel the baby's vigorous reminders of its existence. Now, more than ever before, Holly felt incredibly and desolately alone.

She missed him. Even as remote as he'd been, he'd imbued a sense of security—made her feel protected. Now she felt vulnerable. Afraid. She shook her head and sighed. Must be hormones, she reasoned. Either that or she was going completely nuts, as she'd been to think she could ignore the life burgeoning within her.

Tears pricked at her eyelids as Holly hung her head. She was a useless overemotional wreck. Her feet were swollen, her figure nonexistent, even her moods swung as wildly as the New Zealand flag atop of the Auckland Harbour Bridge. She was about as attractive as an overblown blimp. No wonder Connor didn't want her. Although why he still insisted on sleeping with her she couldn't understand. Maybe she'd move her things into the nanny's bedroom while he was away, she thought, then cast the idea out of hand. She no more wanted to sleep without Connor's solid presence behind her in the bed than she suspected he'd let her indulge in her fit of pique.

The constant ring of the telephone downstairs interrupted her miserable soliloquy. She waited for Thompson to answer it but obviously he was busy elsewhere in the house. She didn't feel like talking to anyone right now. But what if it was Connor? She reached out again and lifted the receiver, at the same time hearing a breathless Thompson pick up from downstairs. She knew she should hang up, but when she heard the caller identify himself as the private investigator she'd engaged, she stayed on the line waiting for him to ask for her.

A flash of hope lit inside her at the sound of his voice. Finally he had some information. The investigation had remained at a frustrating stalemate for far too long, with little more information available other than what she'd grown up knowing. How someone could give birth and raise a child for three years then disappear should have been impossible in a country the size of New Zealand, but somehow, her mother had managed it.

When Holly replaced the receiver a few minutes later she was shaking. The call hadn't been for her. It had been for Connor—to let him know a final report was on its way by boat and, more important, that it held urgent information that Connor had been waiting for.

Holly drew in short sharp breaths through her nose, feeling her chest rise and fall with each intake and exhalation and willed herself to calm down. Had Connor had her investigated as he'd investigated Carla, his ex-wife? Why? And since when?

Anger lit within her, burning with a steady glow. It stood to reason that he'd want to know some background for his baby's lineage. But to order an investigation behind her back? And all along the investigator had been working for both of them—had even deliberately been stonewalling her own repeated requests for more information.

She felt invaded. Violated. And fiercely determined to get to the report before he did. For the first time in days she was glad Connor wasn't around. In fact, right now she wondered if she ever wanted to see him again.

Later, instead of taking her usual afternoon nap, Holly anxiously watched and waited from the master suite's sitting room as Thompson met the courier at the end of the private jetty and accepted a large white envelope. Her heart plummeted. It wasn't very thick. It didn't seem right that something that possibly held the key to her past—her life—could be so insignificant as that single large envelope.

As Thompson made his way back to the house, she shot

silently down the back stairs that led to the informal sitting room. Beyond that lay Connor's office. She hid, poised behind the open door, and listened as Thompson came back inside. He went straight into Connor's office where she heard the tell-tale snick of a key in a lock and the faint slide of wood as he opened then closed a drawer.

That was it? She listened carefully as Thompson left the office again. She replayed the sounds she'd just heard in her head. There'd been no sound of a key being turned in the lock to secure the drawer. Connor would have to beef up his home security if he thought one little drawer would keep her from finding out what secrets lay inside that envelope. A new and more startling thought occurred to her. Had he even planned to share his findings with her? She seriously doubted it.

For an infinitesimal moment she wondered how different her life would be now if she hadn't made love with Connor that night and, even if they had, if she hadn't fallen pregnant? She'd still be at her desk, doing her job better than anyone else could. Still being his trusted right-hand person, instead of someone he now endured only for as long as completely necessary. Holly sighed and pushed her hand against the ache in the small of her back. All the what-ifs in the world wouldn't change anything. She wasn't good enough for Connor Knight. She never would be.

The sound of the French doors being pushed closed caught her attention. Thompson was stepping out for his afternoon walk—a trip she knew would take him at least thirty minutes. Now was her opportunity.

Her heart pounded as she retraced Thompson's steps. If he came back sooner than expected, she'd be clearly visible through the French doors. Holly's hands trembled as she opened the drawer. To her surprise, there was not one, but two identically addressed envelopes. She frowned as she tried to remember exactly what she'd seen from the window upstairs. No, there was nothing wrong with her eyesight. Thompson had definitely received only one. That could only mean one thing—Connor already had a report on her. Holly swiftly removed both envelopes and jammed them under her loose, long-sleeved shirt before heading for the stairs.

On the day bed in the baby's room, she slid her finger under the flap of the already open envelope. Now she had it in her hands, she almost dreaded what the news would disclose, but she had to know. Her hands shook uncontrollably and her heart thundered in her chest, filling her ears with the cacophony, as she tipped the papers from the envelope where they fanned haphazardly onto the lemon-coloured bedcover. She gathered up the loose-leaf typewritten sheets.

The report dated back to just after Christmas and listed, in minute detail, her financial dealings including the regular payments she'd made to the hospital for Andrea. How dare he? He'd obviously requested this information before they even knew she was pregnant. What had he been playing at? She wanted to scream and rant and hit something. Preferably Connor Knight. Holly threw the information back down on the bed in disgust.

All his concern for her when Andrea had died suddenly rang unbelievably false. All along he'd been playing her for a fool. There was only one thing on his mind and that was the baby. Right now, she hated him more than she could have believed, and deep inside, her heart splintered into bleeding shards. Holly's anger drove her to snatch the sealed envelope from the bed. What other secrets had been exposed? Her eyes scanned disappointedly through the first few pages. It was nothing she didn't already know. Summaries of social workers' reports detailed how difficult she'd been to place in a foster home after the incident with the Mitchells' son. Was this all he'd been able to find out?

Holly turned to the next page and instantly her heart shuddered erratically in her chest as she saw the faxed copy of a Police report, dated the twenty-seventh of December nearly twenty-four years ago. Three days after she'd been abandoned.

She sank to the bed, her throat choked with trepidation, and forced herself to continue to read the investigating officer's coldly clinical description of the discovery of a teenage girl's body, dead from a suspected drug overdose, under a motorway overpass. She'd been found wrapped in a bunch of newspapers. A low-resolution copy of the crime scene photo brought a cold metallic taste to Holly's mouth. The dead girl couldn't have been more than seventeen or eighteen. What a waste of a life.

Apparently she'd been found wearing a locket which, when the photo inside was publicised, lead the police back to her family. A family she'd run away from three and a half years earlier.

Fingers shaking, Holly flicked to the report. It was believed the dead girl was Holly's mother—the clue lying in the newspapers that had surrounded the body, many of which shouted the headlines of Holly's abandonment on Christmas Eve in the downtown shopping complex.

Holly pored over the photo again. She could faintly distinguish the headlines he referred to. A gaping sense of loss penetrated her chest and with it a sense of hopelessness. She would never know her mother—could never ask her the million and one questions that had plagued her as a child.

This bereavement felt different from when Andrea had died. This time her sorrow was threaded with frustration and anger at the young woman who'd taken her life and left Holly to a future no one could have known. And yet, the young woman's desolation was painted clear and strong in the picture. Alone and wrapped in the evidence of what had probably been the hardest thing she'd ever done. What could have driven her to such a lonely death? She must have used support services when Holly was born—why hadn't she called for help when she could no longer cope on her own? How had she slipped through the cracks?

No matter what the answers, it was all too late now.

Holly swallowed hard against the lump in her throat. She would not cry. Not again. She'd shed a lifetime of tears for her mother already.

She continued to read, damming all emotion behind an invisible wall, until finally she reached the end and put the papers back into the envelope. Hope flickered like a timid ember in her mind. A woman named Queenie Fleming lived at a coastal holiday spot, about half an hour north of Whangarei. If the investigator's deductions were correct, she could be Holly's grandmother. Her sole surviving relative.

How long would Connor have kept this information from her, Holly wondered. Would he *ever* have told her?

She had to meet Queenie Fleming, although she knew Connor would never sanction such a meeting. Finally, she thought with grim realization, fate was on her side. With Connor away she'd have no difficulty slipping away after her obstetric appointment tomorrow. She could withdraw the money that had been accumulating in her account over the past few months and pay untraceable cash for a rental car. A quiver of excitement ran up her back. Tomorrow she had a date with her past.

"You look tired this morning, miss. Didn't you sleep well?"

"A bit unsettled," she admitted, stifling a yawn.

With forced steadiness, she reluctantly accepted the cup of tea Thompson had poured for her, taking it over to the bay window to look out on the early spring morning. Last night she'd been too excited to sleep, fearful with every creak of the house that Connor had returned. By the time the sun breached the horizon, she'd already been up and dressed and made a last-minute check on the few toiletries and personal items she'd stowed in her bag.

While she'd waited for the next hour to tick past on the bedside clock, she wondered how Connor would react. He'd be livid. By leaving him she was effectively kidnapping his baby. He'd be after her as soon as he could, which was why she had the reports rolled up and secured in the bottom of her bag. Once he discovered she had them, he wouldn't have a leg to stand on. He couldn't force her back here if he tried, and with luck she'd gain a head start of at least a few days.

She didn't doubt he'd come after her, well the baby at least. He loved the baby already with a single-minded intensity she envied. How could he be so certain that he wasn't opening himself up to heartache?

Holly put the cup on the breakfast table and stretched her lower back. She'd been so achy these past couple of days and the baby felt as though it sat lower than before. She'd have to watch her fluid intake today or she'd be forever stopping at restrooms on the way up north. She had to be as invisible as possible. Every stop would leave another imprint of where she'd been and make her easier to find. She'd go light on the liquids.

"The usual toast today?" Thompson asked.

"Yes, please, but I feel like something a bit more substantial. Some scrambled eggs would be lovely." Who knew when she'd next stop to eat?

Thompson hid his surprise well. Since the early days of her

pregnancy when she'd suffered with all-day morning sickness so violently, she'd barely stomached anything heavier than a slice of toast or some fresh fruit for breakfast. But instead of questioning her, he only smiled.

"Coming right up. The helicopter will be here at nine to collect us for your appointment. Mr. Knight will be sorry he missed it."

"He's been busy. I'm sure he'd have been back by now if he could have."

"For certain," Thompson agreed vigorously. "He's so looking forward to the baby."

The enormity of what she was about to do today shafted through her. She couldn't wait until after she'd had the baby, even though she'd given her word to stay until after the birth. In doing what she was about to, she was not only burning her bridges, she was systematically destroying all the roads that led to them, too. Roads that could never be rebuilt at any price. He would never trust her again.

It was a price she was prepared to pay.

Thirteen

Holly swung the car gently around yet another winding curve, her knuckles white, her fingers clenched around the steering wheel.

It had been years since she'd driven, and this road was certainly taking it out of her. Her shoulders sagged in relief as she reached a short straight stretch of road. To the right, a general-goods and fast-food store perched on the corner of an intersection. That must be her turn. She forced her fingers to relax and turned off to the right. As she wound down the hillside, she left banks of green bush behind her as the manuka and native ferns gave way to pasture and the occasional house.

Her back was killing her from sitting so long, but she'd been too scared to pull off the road and take a walk. Driving straight through had been the most sensible thing to do, if not the most comfortable. It had taken three hours by the time she'd deciphered the map and had had to turn back a few times, but finally she was here.

Butterflies buffeted at her stomach as she drove down the main road and straight towards the beach. The road curved to the left, and a tall stand of ancient pohutukawa trees guarded a reserve on the right-hand side. Holly grimaced as a cramp started in her calf muscles. She had to stop and stretch it out before she crippled herself. Thankfully, there were plenty of places to park.

Despite the sunny day, a cool wind blew in off the ocean. Unintentionally she compared the strand of beach, stretching from left to right for a couple of miles, with Connor's secluded private beach on the island. They were nothing alike.

Just as she and Connor were nothing alike, she reminded herself forcefully.

The cramp was getting worse. Holly climbed out of the car and turned to lean against it, stretching out the aggrieved muscles. Despite his aloofness, Connor had taken to massaging her lower legs before bed when he'd realised it helped to prevent the painful cramps that sometimes had her shooting out of bed at night.

She missed him.

God, where had that thought come from? She needed her head read and her mind shrunk. They were poles apart and always would be. She was the daughter of a drug-addicted street kid; he was used to wealth and privilege. Once the baby was born he'd cast her off as easily as he would a shirt with a frayed cuff, although probably with a better reference. There, that felt better. She was angry again.

But her anger didn't last. Holly looked around the reserve and the beach that bordered it. Breakers rolled in, big and fat and just perfect for body surfing. Even at this time of year the place was a miniparadise. In summer it would be magnificent. Why had her mother left? She could only have been a child herself—certainly no more than fifteen.

A group of teenagers burst from the takeaway store across the road, laughing and fooling as they crossed to the reserve and settled at a table where they eagerly started into fresh fish and chips wrapped in newspaper.

Had her mother done this with her friends? Would Holly have done the very same thing if she'd been allowed to grow up here? It was so unfair. She'd been cheated of so many things— a carefree childhood, happy memories, a sense of belonging.

She'd thought she was done with empty questions, but now, here where her mother had been born and raised, she felt them peck at her mind like seagulls picking at a sandwich on the beach.

The reality of actually being here, of walking on a path that her mother had trod was suddenly more overwhelming than Holly had ever imagined—and more frightening. Another flurry of questions, like the swirling sand lifted and cast around by the on-shore breeze, battered at her brain. What if she found her grandmother, and the woman wanted nothing to do with her? What if her mother had had good reason to flee her family and home?

What if she was just setting herself up for rejection again?

A part of her was tempted to get straight back in the rental car and drive flat-out back to Auckland. But she couldn't run away now. She needed to know, for her own sake.

A walk, she needed a walk to clear her head and put some distance between herself and the car that would tempt her to take the easy way out. Besides, a walk would give her a few more minutes to pull her ragged nerves together. Finding her grandmother's house wouldn't be difficult. To the right there weren't more than twenty houses along the beachfront, and the house photo in the report was quite distinctive. She felt sure she'd recognise it from the waterside just as easily as from the road that ran parallel to the beach.

Holly lifted her bag from the front seat, swiped her keys from the ignition and locked the car. At the edge of the beach she kicked off her runners and, balancing against a large park bench, she slipped off her socks and shoved them into her bag. The sand felt cool and soft beneath her feet and she sank a little in the loose granules before she reached the firmer base where the outgoing tide had left its mark scattered with seaweed and pieces of driftwood.

With the setting sun at her back, she headed off down the beach, peering intently at each of the houses she drew level with. The houses were an eclectic collection in various states of size and repair. At a glance it looked as if the traditional Kiwi baches, or holiday homes as they were becoming more widely known, were being superseded by palatial homes that wouldn't have looked out of place in some of Auckland's highly sought-after eastern suburbs. Each one built to face the sea. Holly easily identified her grandmother's tidy cottage from the photo in the report and fought to stem the rush of adrenaline that flooded her body and propelled her up the sand to the wide grass berm that separated the houses from the beach.

Her heart hammered against her ribs as Holly placed a shaking hand on the front gate and gently pushed it open. This side of the house was built to enjoy the vista of the bay, and wide French doors were flung open. Holly determinedly placed one foot in front of the other until she was standing on the weathered deck and raised her hand to knock firmly on the doorjamb.

Her heart skipped a beat as she heard a noise from inside,

but still no one came at her knock. She banged against the door frame again.

"Hello?" An elderly man's head popped up from the other side of the fence that bordered the property. "If you're looking for Queenie she's coming up the beach now."

"Yes, yes, I am. Thank you."

"Say, you look familiar. Have I seen you before?"

Holly's breath caught in her throat. "No, I've never been here before." She swiftly descended the shallow stairs that led off the deck and walked back down to the beach, scanning the shoreline for the figure that was in all probability her only living family.

All at once she felt the earth tilt. The woman walking towards her was older than the photo from the locket that had been printed in the paper, but the likeness was unmistakable.

Queenie Fleming. Her grandmother.

Holly's shoes dropped unheeded from her hands as she stopped and stared, unable to speak. Unable to even think.

"Hello? Were you looking for me?"

For longer than you can ever know. "Yes, I am." Holly managed to force the words past lips that quivered as they stretched into a welcoming smile.

As she drew nearer, the woman's smile became more set and her face, weathered by sun and wind and marked with lines of sorrow, paled as she fixed her gaze on Holly. "Giselle? No, you can't be…" Her voice trailed away weakly.

A shiver rippled through her—Giselle, her mother. It was all she could do not to throw herself in the other woman's arms, yet one remaining ounce of caution—a lingering fear of being brushed aside if she identified who she was—held her in place.

"I'm sorry, dear, you startled me. You look such a lot like

my late daughter. Don't worry about a silly old thing like me." She gathered herself together and gave Holly another smile. "You look worn-out, dear. Long trip? Why don't you come and have a cuppa with me. I'm Queenie Fleming, but the young ones around here call me Nana, you may as well, too."

Queenie's chatter washed over her, and Holly felt herself nod, not even believing it could be so simple. *Nana.* Her stomach did a little flip. If she'd grown up here she'd have had every right to call her Nana.

"Wait, please?" She put a hand out to the woman's arm, her fingers curling gently around it ever so briefly before letting go. Her grandmother. It still seemed unreal.

"Am I going too fast for you, dear? Oh look, you've left your shoes in the sand. The tide'll take them if you're not careful." She bustled back and collected Holly's shoes. "Come on with me and I'll sit you down and get you a nice hot cuppa. Gee, this wind has some bite in it, doesn't it?"

Without hesitation Nana hooked an arm around Holly's expanded waist, helped her over the loose sand and towards the old but well-maintained house that squatted amongst the larger architecturally designed homes.

"They call it progress, dear." Her grandmother sniffed and waved a disparaging hand towards the two-storied home to the side, leaving no doubt as to what she thought of it, and led Holly across the deck and into the cottage. "I call it a shame."

"I can see why. It's so beautiful here."

"I've lived here over sixty years, was born and grew up in the area. I never thought I'd see the day when my neighbours would be city folk weekending at the beach. Ah well, one thing you can't control and that's time. When I'm gone, no doubt this place will be bowled and another place built—it's not like I've any family to leave it to. Sit down there, dear. You'll be comfortable on the firm chair."

"Thanks." Holly sank gratefully into a roomy and blessedly comfortable wicker chair. "You're on your own?"

"Yes, just me left. That's why you'll have to indulge an old woman who doesn't get a lot of company. I tend to talk far too much when I do." She laughed and slapped her hips at the joke. "My husband, Ted, passed on five years ago. It's been a bit lonely since then." She gave a wink and tenderly patted Holly's belly. "You won't be alone for long. You look about fit to pop anyday."

Holly smiled, trying not to dwell on another loss—the grandfather she'd never know. "I'm supposed to be another three weeks yet."

"You'll be early, you mark my words. Have you thought of any names yet?" Nana filled the kettle and put it on to boil, before clattering about in a cupboard and getting cups and spooning tealeaves into a pot.

"No, I haven't." She hadn't let herself. She didn't dare to.

"Don't worry. You'll think of something perfect when the time is right. Now, my Giselle, she was a determined one. So set in her thoughts. Nothing could sway her. She always said that if she had a little girl she'd name her Holly." Queenie sighed sadly. "She died twenty-four years ago this coming Christmas and I still don't know what we did wrong there."

"Wrong? Why?" Ice traced a nervous finger down Holly's spine.

"We were older parents. She came as a late bonus in our marriage, and as a result we probably overindulged her. At least Ted said *I* did. He put his foot down when she started to hang out with a young larrikin from further up the coast. Nice family, shame about the boy. Mind you, he settled down some in later years. Anyway, Ted made it quite clear that he disapproved of young Matt and forbade her from seeing him again. One night, soon after, she ran away from home. She was just shy of her fifteenth birthday. We did our best to locate her, but the police said some kids simply don't want to be found. We never did find out what drove her away in the end. It broke my Ted's heart. He was never the same."

Holly felt faint and forced herself to drag much-needed air into her lungs. Her voice shaking, she replied. "Maybe I know."

"You know? Why would you know, dear?" Nana gave Holly a puzzled smile before turning back to the whistling kettle and filling the teapot with hot water.

"I think I know why she ran away." Holly gripped the cane arms of her chair so hard she thought she'd snap them into matchsticks. "I'm Holly."

"That's nice, dear. Born at Christmas were you?" Slowly realization dawned on the older woman's face, and shock replaced her friendly smile. Her skin paled, driving the lifetime of sunshine from her weathered visage, and her eyes rounded in disbelief.

She should have been more careful, Holly thought, more considerate of the older woman's feelings. But she'd waited so damn long that suddenly even another second was forever.

Queenie lowered herself carefully into a chair opposite Holly. She opened, then closed, her mouth a few times before one word shuddered past her thin lips. "H-Holly?"

"Yes." Holly's voice was barely a whisper as it fought past the tears that constricted her throat. "I think Giselle was my mother."

Nana clapped her fingers to her mouth in a futile attempt to stifle the moan that escaped. "A baby? She had a baby?

That's why she ran away?" Tears began to track down her wrinkled cheeks. "But how did she cope? What did she do? Oh mercy, why didn't she tell us?"

Holly could only shake her head. "I don't know. Somehow she looked after me. Then on Christmas Eve, my third birthday, she left me where I'd be found and cared for. I suppose she didn't really know what else to do. I don't remember her face, but I remember a tune she used to sing." Holly started to hum the song she'd sung to herself over and over again at night to keep fear away, until one night she'd realised that no one was ever coming to get her and she'd locked the tune down deep in her memory. She stopped when Nana rose abruptly from her chair and left the room, coming back a few seconds later, a music box in her hands.

"It was my mother's. Giselle always loved it." Slowly she turned the key on the side before opening the box. Holly's skin prickled as the tune swelled through the air. *Her tune.*

The music box ran out and silence filled the room before Holly slid from her chair and knelt, wrapping her arms around her grandmother's waist and placing her head in her lap.

"I thought I'd never find you," she whispered brokenly against the soft fabric of her Nana's dress, finally giving way to the decades of loneliness that could now, finally, begin to be assuaged.

Her grandmother rested a hand on Holly's head, stroking trembling fingers soothingly through the long dark tresses, her voice awash with emotion. "I'm so glad you did, my darling. I'm so glad you did."

The next morning Holly awoke to the sound of seagulls calling across the beach and waves crawling up the sand. Although she'd slept deeply, she still felt exhausted. After dinner last night she and her grandmother had walked back to her car together, and Holly had garaged it at the cottage. Then they'd talked into the small hours of the night, piecing together the life they'd been cheated of. And yet, despite all she'd never had a chance to know before now, Holly couldn't blame her mother. She'd been young and foolish, following a dream of love with a boy she knew her father didn't approve of. How she'd hung on to Holly for as long as she did was a miracle in itself.

On Nana's part, while she couldn't come to grips with the fact that her daughter had never asked her family for help, she was so incredibly happy to have Holly here with her. Finally Holly had somewhere she belonged, someone of her own to love. And Nana was so excited about the new baby, Holly hadn't had the heart, or the courage, to tell her the truth last night. But she would have to do it today.

When she finally summoned the courage, her grandmother's eyes had filled with tears of compassion.

"But you love this Connor Knight, don't you?" Nana asked, confusion clear in her eyes.

"Yes." It was the simple truth, and Holly couldn't deny it to the woman who deserved honesty from her above all else.

"Does he know?"

"No, I've never told him."

"Well then, maybe you should think about that."

"I couldn't. If I told him now he'd only think I'm doing it to stay with the baby." Holly looked down at her hands. "I didn't want this baby. Not at the beginning. Not even a week ago. Not knowing my family, and with Andrea—I've been so scared."

"Well, now you know. There are no hidden nasties amongst our lot. You have to let go of the things you can't control, dear. Your baby will be fine. You'll see."

"It's too late." Holly's voice was flat, devoid of emotion as if the past twenty-four hours had stripped her bare.

"What do you mean? How can it ever be too late? Look at us. Yesterday I didn't even know you existed, yet I love you as if I'd been a part of your life since the day you were born," Queenie argued passionately.

Dread filled Holly's heart. How would her grandmother take the news? How could she understand? "I've already signed away all parental rights to Connor. Under the agreement, I won't even see it after it's born." Her voice cracked on a sob as the truth rammed home. She would never see her baby. Never be a part of its life, never hear its first words, or see its first hesitant steps. Never be party to her baby's first day at school, or its first wiggly tooth. *What had she done?* She didn't think she could hurt any more, but now she felt as though she'd scraped away the very lining of her soul.

Queenie's face dropped and she gathered Holly into the comfort of her arms. "Oh, my darling. My poor, poor girl. Don't you worry—we'll sort something out. You have family now. I might not be much, but I'm yours and we'll fight this together."

"It's hopeless, Nana. The contract is unbreakable. He's made certain of that. It's what he does. Who he is." Holly pulled away and stood apart, her shoulders slumped, her head low. She could hardly bear the truth herself—the bitter and cruel irony—that she should want this baby now more than anything she'd wanted before. "There's nothing we can do."

"You're wrong, Holly. You can't give up. I won't let you. You haven't waited all this time to be a quitter now. Why don't you go out and enjoy that sunshine and take a walk along the beach before the rain comes. I have some phone calls to make."

"I'll wait for you." Holly didn't want to be alone with her thoughts. Not now.

"No, dear, you go on. Once I've made those calls I'm going to look out some old photos of Giselle you might like to keep."

"I can stay and help you."

"No, no, dear. This is something I have to do for myself. Now hurry on before the rain, my old bones never lie."

Understanding dawned. In meeting her, her Nana finally had some of the answers she'd sought, and while neither of them would ever know the full story, it was time for her to make her peace with her daughter. And time for Holly to try and make peace with her own choices, she realised with hollow truth sounding a knell deep inside.

The tide was full out on the beach, and Holly was amazed at the width of firm damp sand. Her feet felt invigorated as the ground shells crunched beneath her feet and, in the damper spots, squelched up in between her toes. She wished her back felt as good. The nagging ache from yesterday had escalated into a dragging dull pain. Maybe her bones were becoming a weather forecaster like her grandmother's. She smiled softly to herself at the thought of having a familial link for the first time.

In the distance Holly saw a flock of birds scatter off the point. She laughed aloud as they wheeled in the air, their angry cries at being disturbed carried down the beach. Then, suddenly, her laughter died on her lips. A familiar sound beat at the air, drowning out the birds and sending deepening dread from her heart all the way to the soles of her feet.

The dark shape of a helicopter swooped over the hills at the end of the beach.

"No!" she shouted. "Not yet. It's too soon."

She turned and struggled through the sand, desperate to get back to her grandmother's. Desperate to find sanctuary.

She flung a look over her shoulder. A short distance away

the Agusta set down on the hard-packed sand and an all-too-recognizable figure stepped down.

"Holly! Stop!"

"No-o-o!" she cried. "Go away. I don't want you here. Leave me alone."

Connor was at her side quickly. She felt his presence before he stepped around her, halting her in her frantic flight.

Strong. Powerful. Angry.

"What the hell did you think you were doing?" he demanded.

"How can you even ask me that? Like you were going to tell me and bring me on a family visit? I don't think so. How could you keep something that important from me? I had a right to know! Oh!" She heard a soft pop and a warm gush of fluid rushed between her legs.

"Your waters?" Connor scooped her into his arms. "Don't worry. I'll get you to the chopper. I'll have you back in Auckland in no time."

"No! Put me down." Holly struggled against him, forcing him to let her feet back down to touch the sand. "Ahhhh." Holly clutched at his forearms and groaned as the dragging pain in the small of her back intensified and spread around the front of her belly, tightening and tightening, then slowly easing off. "I'm not going anywhere."

"Holly, you have to." For the first time in her life, Holly saw Connor at a disadvantage. Her groan of pain sent fear rushing into his eyes.

"I've waited a lifetime to be here. I'm not leaving now."

"You can bring my granddaughter back to my house, young man." Queenie strode down the beach towards them, a fiercely protective expression on her face.

"Nana! It's too early. What if there's something wrong?"

"My point exactly." Connor interjected. "Look, I can have

you at Auckland hospital in close to half an hour." Connor rested his hands on Holly's hips, looking her straight in the eye. "Please, Holly. Let me take you back."

"You don't need to be frightened, my darling," Nana interrupted. "We've birthed many a baby here." She turned and fixed a stern look at Connor. "Bring her to the house and then make yourself useful. You can call the local doctor for me."

"She's coming back to Auckland." Connor looked from one woman to the other. This was his baby they were talking about, and this woman—Holly's grandmother, he corrected himself—expected him to simply let them have the baby here? They were out of their minds.

"It's starting again." Holly clutched hold of his arms again, this time breathing through the contraction.

"You really don't have time, Mr. Knight. The women in our family have our babies mighty quick."

In the face of her testimonial and Holly's frighteningly quick onset of labour, Connor couldn't argue any longer. He lifted Holly back into his arms and followed her grandmother.

Half an hour later he paced back from the beach after reluctantly sending the helicopter off to the nearest grassed landing area, hopefully to await his call to return and take Holly and the baby back to Auckland. He let himself into the house and strode into Holly's room. "Where's the damn doctor?" he growled. "I rang him ages ago."

"It hasn't been that long," Holly answered, her hair already beginning to mat against her forehead as perspiration built up on her face. "Here comes another one. Ahhhh."

"Come here and rub her back like this, nice and firm." Nana took Connor's hand and pressed it against Holly's back. "No, no, lad. Not like that. That'll never give her any relief. Firm, like this."

Finally he seemed to be doing something right in the old woman's eyes. Holly sat back to front on a tall wooden-backed chair, her arms resting along the top rail, her legs spread on either side. He sensed her body tighten and spasm, could feel the moment she separated her mind from her surroundings and focused one hundred percent on the process that wracked her body.

This wasn't as simple as negotiating a contract. Nothing quantified how helpless he felt. He was responsible for what she was going through right now.

As she sighed a moan of relief, Connor acknowledged he should have cared a lot more. Should have listened to his inner voice when it urged him to let himself love her.

He'd been coming through Auckland Customs when his cell phone had buzzed with the frantic call from Thompson, who'd discovered Holly's flight from the obstetrician's rooms yesterday. He hadn't had time to be angry. All he'd felt was fear. Fear that something would happen to Holly.

On the periphery of his thoughts he heard another man's voice. The doctor, at last. Connor stepped aside to let him introduce himself to Holly.

"How're the pains?" the doctor asked.

"Awful," Holly replied with a weak grin, before closing her eyes and breathing through the next wave.

"I think it's time we got you up onto the bed so I can examine you."

"Oh!" Holly gasped, "I feel like I need to push."

"Hold back as much as you can. We need to check you first."

Connor and Queenie swiftly helped Holly onto the bed while the doctor slipped away to wash his hands and glove up. Once back he quickly examined her before giving her a smile and a nod. "You're all set to go."

"Connor!" Holly shrieked his name. He was at her side in a second, and she gripped his hand so tight his fingers lost all feeling. But the discomfort was minor as he became lost in another more miraculous event. The birth of his baby.

He couldn't tell later if it had been minutes or hours, but the incredible rush of seeing his son slide from Holly's body beat all description. The doctor lifted the squalling infant onto Holly's stomach, and Connor reached out to touch his son.

His son! The gift of life he'd never thought would be his.

Tears coursed down Holly's cheeks as she looked at the child, but she didn't reach to hold him, instead she turned her cheek against the stack of pillows bunched behind her and closed her eyes.

"Look at him, Holly. He's perfect. We have a son." His voice broke with emotion.

"No. Take him." Her voice shook.

"Wh-what?" Had he heard her correctly?

"Take him. He's yours. You have what you wanted. Take him now." The harsh whisper that dragged from her throat slashed him to his core. "Take him before I can't bear to let him go."

The doctor and Holly's grandmother exchanged worried glances as they attended to the final stages of the birth.

"Now, now, girl. That's no way to talk," her grandmother admonished gently. "Look at him. He's beautiful."

"I don't want him. Please, take him away." Her voice rose in pitch, and the doctor reached forward to swaddle the baby in a receiving blanket and gave Connor a troubled look.

Connor nodded in reply. "Take him out of the room. We need to talk."

Tremors shook Holly's body as the doctor handed the baby

to Nana, who cradled him close, then swiftly covered his patient with a sheet and woollen blankets. "Keep her warm, she's in shock. We'll be just outside the door."

As they closed the door behind them, Connor lowered himself carefully on the bed. Still Holly kept her face pressed against the pillows, away from him.

"Why don't you just take him and go?" Her voice, muffled against the pillow, wrenched a gaping hole in his chest.

"I can't go. Not without you."

"You don't need me. You have him now. It's what you wanted isn't it?"

"Did you think I'd just toss you a cheque, pick up the baby and go? What kind of man do you think I am? It's not about the baby anymore, Holly. I want *you*, and I'm not leaving here without you."

She turned back to face him, her mouth a twisted line. "No-o-o! You can't do that to me. You can't demand any more from me. I've done everything you asked. Now go, and leave me alone."

"Holly, you can't abandon him like this. Don't do this to yourself. Don't do this to our baby." Maybe shock tactics would work, he thought, grasping at anything he could to shake her from her resolve. "I read the report on your mother; it was faxed it to me in the States. Haven't you wondered if she died that way because she couldn't bear to be without you? Didn't you learn anything from her death? Don't you see? You're doing exactly what she did, except she was too young and too alone to know how it could be any different. Give yourself a chance. Give our son a chance."

"How dare you. She had no choice. I made mine," she whispered, her face paling. "I pity the poor woman you fall in love with, Connor Knight, I hope she never knows how low or how mean you're prepared to go." He barely made out her words through the thickness of her tears.

"Then pity yourself," he answered, finding her hand beneath the covers and holding it firmly in his.

"Don't! Don't lie to me."

"I mean it, Holly. I love you." He reached forward and brushed her damp hair from her face, his fingers tingling at the softness of her skin. "I've been a complete fool. I didn't tell you about the investigation because I didn't want you to have an excuse to leave. I wanted you to need me. I wanted to be the only one there for you, even though I fought it and fought it and treated you abominably every step of the way. I couldn't even admit it to myself until last week. I knew I needed to talk to you before the baby arrived but I couldn't do it over the phone. How could I tell you from thousands of miles away that I love you? You have every right to never want to forgive me."

She remained silent; her eyes boring into his as if she could see right through him, as if nothing he said mattered. Connor held her gaze and felt his heart skip a beat. He'd missed her with a physical and emotional ache that he hadn't wanted to identify when he'd first arrived in the States. He'd thrown himself into business and meetings, but in the back of his mind, and during every quiet moment, he'd wondered and worried about Holly. What kind of day she'd had. How she was feeling. Did she miss him as much as he missed her?

Bit by bit, he'd recognised that his motivation to close the deal and get home was no longer the imminent birth of his baby.

He wanted Holly. He wanted her like he had never wanted any woman.

It shamed him to realise it had taken the distance of several thousand miles to allow himself to admit he loved her. Right now, nothing he'd achieved in his career, in his entire life, meant a thing if he couldn't convince Holly of that too.

"Do you know why I wanted this baby, our baby, so much?" he asked, leaning forward to gently rest his forehead against hers. When she didn't respond he continued, regardless. "On your birthday last year I discovered Carla had terminated a pregnancy in the early stages of our marriage. It doesn't excuse what I did, but when you became pregnant all I could see was that I had another chance. A chance to do it right this time. Maybe, in the back of my mind, I even wanted you to fall pregnant.

"I put you through months of hell for my own selfish reasons, to replace the baby she killed. I couldn't let another child of mine die like that. When you talked about 'options' at Carmen's office that day, I was incensed. What if you'd insisted on a termination? My fears made me pretend you were just like her, when deep down I should have known better. Known you could never be anything like her."

"She had an abortion?" Holly asked, her voice hushed and filled with disbelief.

"Without ever telling me—then she was sterilised to make certain it would never happen again." Connor drew back and looked deep into her eyes, relieved to see the anguish had begun to fade, that the tears had finally dried. "Holly, you were right. I did treat you like nothing more than an incubator. By dehumanising you I didn't need to face my own feelings or inadequacies. I couldn't help my first baby, couldn't stop its murder. I was prepared to do anything to make sure that never happened again. Can you ever forgive me? Can you ever love me?"

"Love you? I've loved you forever, Connor Knight. It was killing me slowly inside working with you, then living with you, and knowing you were unattainable. I felt so alone, so unwanted. That night we made love? I wanted you so much. Making love with you gave me a chance to pretend that you wanted me, too."

"Holly, you didn't need to pretend. I needed you that night more than I'd ever needed another human being in my entire life. You were so real. So giving. So beautiful."

"And so wrong for you. When I saw you with your family the next day, I knew I could never be good enough for you. I had no background, no family. And at the office party, you obviously loved children. It was there in every movement, every gesture you made with the children. I couldn't give you that. My fear made that impossible."

"Nothing is impossible. Not for us. Not anymore. I love you, Holly Christmas. Will you marry me?"

"Marry you?" Her breath squeezed tight in her lungs. Her hands shook. "You don't need to marry me. What will your father say? What about your brothers?"

"They'll tell me again what a fool I was not to have married you before our child came into this world. In fact, they're barely speaking to me, they've been so disgusted with my actions. So, do you have an answer for me, my beautiful Holly?"

"Nothing would make me happier." She reached for him, a burst of pure joy blooming deep in her chest, chasing away the last pockets of darkness, of fear, of loneliness.

"So what do you say you reintroduce yourself to our little man." Connor tipped his head towards the door through which the newborn's demanding cries could be heard. "Something tells me he wants to meet his mama."

"Please! Bring him back."

Connor rose from the bed and swung open the door, putting his arms out to take the baby, his heart filled to bursting at the feel of this tiny adorable infant in his arms. Gently he gave him to Holly and watched, a lump forming in his throat as the baby settled in her arms and she pushed away the blanket and checked his long slender fingers tipped with perfect nails and his tiny pink toes, before gathering him to her and pressing her lips against his little face.

"He is perfect, isn't he?" Her voice was full of wonder.

"Yes, yes he is. And so are you. Thank you for the gift of my son."

"Poor little guy, he needs a name," she said softly, a gentle smile of wonder curving her lips as she gazed upon his tiny face.

"Why don't we call him André, for his aunty."

"André." Holly tested the sound of the name on her tongue. "Thank you. Andrea would have loved that."

Epilogue

"Have I told you how beautiful you look today, Mrs. Knight?"

"Only about three dozen times." Holly smiled as she leaned into her husband, relishing the hard strength of his body against hers and feeling the embers of desire stir deep within.

Their wedding guests had departed on Tony Knight's luxury yacht and into the crisp clear winter night, and with them, André. It would be their first time without him. She'd objected, but his doting grandfather had insisted that he and Queenie, who was staying at his house for the weekend, could manage just fine.

She still couldn't believe the chubby little boy was theirs, or that he'd been an active and demanding part of their lives for nine months now. Soon he'd be walking, no doubt making Thompson's life far more complicated than he'd ever bargained for.

But tonight wasn't about André. Tonight was about Connor and her.

She reached up and pulled her husband's face closer to hers, inhaling his scent, making it a part of her as much as she was now a part of him.

"Have I told you today how much I love you, Mr. Knight?"

Connors lips parted in a smile. "Only about three dozen times."

He closed the gap between them, taking her lips with a fierce possession Holly savoured with soul-deep satisfaction and the embers flamed into urgent need.

As they drew apart and slowly walked back to the house, Holly looked up at him, her eyes aglow with the joy of the truth that filled her heart every day.

Finally she had her very own family.

Finally her life was complete.

* * * * *

Don't miss THE CEO'S CONTRACT BRIDE,
Declan Knight's romance,
available in January 2007 from
Yvonne Lindsay and Silhouette Desire!

A special treat for you from Harlequin Blaze!

Turn the page for a sneak preview of
DECADENT
by
New York Times *bestselling author*
Suzanne Forster

Available November 2006,
wherever series books are sold.

Harlequin Blaze—Your ultimate destination
for red-hot reads.
With six titles every month, you'll never guess
what you'll discover under the covers…

RUN, ALLY! Don't be fooled by him. He's evil. Don't let him touch you!

But as the forbidding figure came through the mists toward her, Ally knew she couldn't run. His features burned with dark malevolence, and his physical domination of everything around him seemed to hold her like a net.

She'd heard the tales. She knew all about the Wolverton legend and the ghost that haunted The Willows, an elegant old mansion lost by Micha Wolverton nearly a hundred years ago. According to folklore, the estate was stolen from the Wolvertons, and Micha was killed, trying to reclaim it. His dying vow was to be reunited with the spirit of his beloved wife, who'd taken her life for reasons no one would speak of, except in whispers. But Ally had never put much stock in the fantasy. She didn't believe in ghosts.

Until now—

She still didn't understand what was happening. The figure

had materialized out of the mist that lay thick on the damp cemetery soil. A cool breeze and silvery moonlight had played against the ancient stone of the crypts surrounding her, until they joined the mist, causing his body to thicken and solidify right before her eyes. That was when she realized she'd seen this man before. Or thought she had, at least.

His face was familiar…so familiar, yet she couldn't put it together. Not with him looming so near. She stepped back as he approached.

"Don't be afraid," he said. His voice wasn't what she expected. It didn't sound as if it were coming from beyond the grave. It was deep and sensual. Commanding.

"Who are you?" she managed.

"You should know. You summoned me."

"No, I didn't." She had no idea what he was talking about. Two minutes ago, she'd been crouching behind a moss-covered crypt, spying on the mansion that had once been The Willows, but was now Club Casablanca. And then this—

If he was Micah, he might be angry that she was trespassing on his property. "I'll go," she said. "I won't come back. I promise."

"You're not going anywhere."

Words snagged in her throat. "Wh-why not? What do you want?"

"If I wanted something, Ally, I'd take it. This is about need."

His words resonated as he moved within inches of her. She tried to back away, but her feet were useless. "And you need something from me?"

"Good guess." His tone burned with irony. "I need lips, soft and surrendered, a body limp with desire."

"My lips, my bod—?"

"Only yours."

"Why? Why me?" This couldn't be Micha. He didn't want any woman but Rose. He'd died trying to get back to her.

"Because you want that, too," he said.

Wanted what? A ghost of her own? She'd always found the legend impossibly romantic, but how could he have known that? How could he know anything about her? Besides, she'd sworn off inappropriate men, and what could be more inappropriate than a ghost? She shook her head again, still not willing to admit the truth. But her heart wouldn't play along. It clattered inside her chest. The mere thought of his kiss, his touch, terrified her. This wildness, it was fear, wasn't it?

When his fingertips touched her cheek, she flinched, expecting his flesh to be cold, lifeless. It was anything but that. His skin was smooth and hot, gentle, yet demanding. And while his dark brown eyes were filled with mystery and wonder, there was a sensitivity about them that threatened to disarm her if she looked too deeply.

"These lips are mine," he said, as if stating a universal fact that she was helpless to avoid. In truth, it was just that. She couldn't stop him.

And she didn't want to.

Find out how the story unfolds in…
DECADENT
by
New York Times *bestselling author*
Suzanne Forster.
On sale November 2006.

Harlequin Blaze—Your ultimate destination
for red-hot reads.
With six titles every month, you'll never guess
what you'll discover under the covers…

REQUEST YOUR FREE BOOKS!

2 FREE NOVELS PLUS 2 FREE GIFTS!

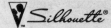

Passionate, Powerful, Provocative!

YES! Please send me 2 FREE Silhouette Desire® novels and my 2 FREE gifts. After receiving them, if I don't wish to receive any more books, I can return the shipping statement marked "cancel." If I don't cancel, I will receive 6 brand-new novels every month and be billed just $3.80 per book in the U.S., or $4.47 per book in Canada, plus 25¢ shipping and handling per book and applicable taxes, if any*. That's a savings of almost 15% off the cover price! I understand that accepting the 2 free books and gifts places me under no obligation to buy anything. I can always return a shipment and cancel at any time. Even if I never buy another book from Silhouette, the two free books and gifts are mine to keep forever.

225 SDN EEXJ 326 SDN EEXU

Name	(PLEASE PRINT)
Address	Apt.
City	State/Prov.	Zip/Postal Code

Signature (if under 18, a parent or guardian must sign)

Mail to Silhouette Reader Service™:

IN U.S.A.	**IN CANADA**
P.O. Box 1867	P.O. Box 609
Buffalo, NY	Fort Erie, Ontario
14240-1867	L2A 5X3

Not valid to current Silhouette Desire subscribers.

Want to try two free books from another line?
Call 1-800-873-8635 or visit www.morefreebooks.com.

* Terms and prices subject to change without notice. NY residents add applicable sales tax. Canadian residents will be charged applicable provincial taxes and GST. This offer is limited to one order per household. All orders subject to approval. Credit or debit balances in a customer's account(s) may be offset by any other outstanding balance owed by or to the customer. Please allow 4 to 6 weeks for delivery.

SDES06

SAVE UP TO $30! SIGN UP TODAY!

INSIDE *Romance*

The complete guide to your favorite
Harlequin®, Silhouette® and Love Inspired® books.

✓ Newsletter ABSOLUTELY FREE! No purchase necessary.

✓ Valuable coupons for future purchases of Harlequin,
  Silhouette and Love Inspired books in every issue!

✓ Special excerpts & previews in each issue. Learn about all
  the hottest titles before they arrive in stores.

✓ No hassle—mailed directly to your door!

✓ Comes complete with a handy shopping checklist
  so you won't miss out on any titles.

- -

SIGN ME UP TO RECEIVE INSIDE ROMANCE
ABSOLUTELY FREE
(Please print clearly)

_____
Name

_____
Address

_____
City/Town   State/Province   Zip/Postal Code

(098 KKM EJL9)

Please mail this form to:
In the U.S.A.: Inside Romance, P.O. Box 9057, Buffalo, NY 14269-9057
In Canada: Inside Romance, P.O. Box 622, Fort Erie, ON L2A 5X3
OR visit http://www.eHarlequin.com/insideromance

IRNBPA06R   ® and ™ are trademarks owned and used by the trademark owner and/or its licensee.

Silhouette Desire

COMING NEXT MONTH

#1759 THE EXPECTANT EXECUTIVE—Kathie DeNosky
The Elliotts
An Elliott heiress's unexpected pregnancy is the subject of high-society gossip. Wait till the baby's father finds out!

#1760 THE SUBSTITUTE MILLIONAIRE—Susan Mallery
The Million Dollar Catch
What is a billionaire to do when he discovers the woman he's been hiding his true identity from is carrying his child?

#1761 BEDDED *THEN* WED—Heidi Betts
Marrying his neighbor's daughter is supposed to be merely a business transaction…until he finds himself falling for his convenient wife.

**#1762 SCANDALS FROM THE THIRD BRIDE—
Sara Orwig**
The Wealthy Ransomes
Bought by the highest bidder, a bachelorette has no recourse but to spend the evening with the man who once left her at the altar.

#1763 THE PREGNANCY NEGOTIATION—Kristi Gold
She is desperate to get pregnant. And her playboy neighbor is just the right man for the job.

**#1764 HOLIDAY CONFESSIONS—
Anne Marie Winston**
True love may be blind…but can it withstand the lies between them?

SDCNM1006